Eerie Tales
from Old Korea

Eerie Tales from Old Korea

Published by Seoul Selection
4199 Campus Dr., Suite 550
Irvine, CA 92612, USA
Tel: 949-509-6584
Fax: 949-509-6599
E-mail: publisher@seoulselection.com
Website: www.seoulselection.com

ISBN: 978-1-62412-002-2
Library of Congress Control Number: 2013938372

Printed in the Republic of Korea

Eerie Tales
from Old Korea

Compiled by
Brother Anthony of Taizé

CONTENTS

Introduction _7

PART I

A Beggar's Wages _15
A Hunter's Mistake _22
The Donkey Maker _24
A Submarine Adventure _27
Necessity, the Mother of Invention _33
The Essence of Life _41
The Goose That Laid the Golden Egg _44
An Aesculapian Episode _48
Cats and the Dead _57
A Korean Jonah _60
A Brave Governor _63
Hen Versus Centipede _67
A Tiger Hunter's Revenge _74
How Jin Outwitted the Devils _82
The Ghost of a Ghost _90
The Tenth Scion _96

PART II

The Story of Jang Doryeong _105
Yun Se-Pyeong, the Wizard _112
The Literary Man of Imsil _115
The Man on the Road _118
The Man Who Became a Pig _121
The Grateful Ghost _124
Ten Thousand Devils _127
The Home of the Fairies _133
The Snake's Revenge _146
The Brave Magistrate _149
The King of Hell _152
Hong's Experiences in Hades _157
Ta-hong _163

Publisher's Note

We tried to preserve the original translations of the stories insofar as it was possible but have made some edits for the convenience of the contemporary reader. For the romanization of Korean words and names, we have applied the Revised Romanization method instead of the McCune-Reischauer system that was used in the original text.

Introduction

The nineteenth century was particularly fond of ghost stories. We only have to recall Charles Dickens's *A Christmas Carol* to be reminded of this, and there are many other British and American writers of ghost stories whose names might be cited. The missionaries who came to Korea toward the end of the nineteenth century were no exception to this fondness, but for many years they were assured by the Korean scholars they questioned that no such stories existed in Korea. Eventually, they discovered that Korea too had its supply of ghosts, but because the stories seemed too frivolous or connected with shamanism and Buddhism, the scholars had been ashamed to tell them that they existed.

In actual fact, a main source of such tales proved to be the collections of *yadam* written by scholars. *Yadam* was a form of short tale originating in China and was very popular in Korea later in the Joseon period. The topics were extremely varied; the *yadam* featured stories about a great variety of social milieux and human types. Entertainment was clearly the main purpose.

Whereas the Confucian classics and Chinese-character poetry were the gateway to officialdom and the proof of scholarly excellence, the *yadam* offered an escape valve for a desire to be closer to daily life. The stories told in *yadam* were about individuals who were not always admirable paragons of Confucian virtue; rather, they were often artful dodgers who managed to escape from tricky situations, survive traps, deal with problems, and generally survive. The *yadam* were set in towns, frequently humorous or satirical, and often peopled by low-class, uneducated, poverty-stricken characters. Among them were tales of ghosts, spirits, monsters, paradise, and the underworld. The links to Taoism, Buddhism, and Shamanism are soon obvious.

The missionaries who came to Korea after 1884 were obliged to teach themselves not only the Korean spoken language but also the Classical Chinese that at that time was the official language of administration, scholarship, and almost all literary activity in Korea. Some of the first missionaries mastered both languages to a remarkable degree and began to translate texts written in Classical Chinese into English. The names of Homer B. Hulbert and James Scarth Gale are well known, and both men were outstanding scholars. Both of them were born early in 1863 and arrived in Korea in the late 1880s.

The role played by Hulbert in support of Korean independence in the years prior to Japan's final annexation—when Japan was taking control of Korea—is well known in Korea. It culminated in his being sent by the Emperor to the Second International Peace Conference, to be held in The Hague in June 1907. After that he was unable to return to live in Korea. In the 1890s, a monthly magazine—the *Korean Repository*—was established by the missionaries to publish short articles about many aspects of Korean life and culture. It ceased to appear in 1899, and then, in 1901, Homer Hulbert established another monthly, the *Korea Review*, with much the same aim. It was published every month until the end of 1905, just as Japan reduced Korea to a Japanese protectorate. While a number of missionaries contributed to the *Repository*, almost everything in the *Review* was written by Hulbert, and for the first four years it carried portions of his deeply researched "History of Korea" each month, which mainly consisted of old Korean sources translated from the original Classical Chinese. However, each number also contained extensive extracts from the local newspapers, articles about various aspects of Korean life, and, occasionally, from 1902, Korean ghost stories. Presumably, these were mostly translated by Hulbert, but with the exception of "The

Tenth Scion," which was translated by Rev. G. Engel, he gives no source for them.

James Gale was more deeply interested in literature than Hulbert, and correspondingly less in politics. When Gale published his "History of Korea" in the monthly magazine *Korea Mission Field* in the 1920s, it was full of quotations of the poetry written (in Classical Chinese) by ancient scholars and ministers. Unlike Hulbert, who was an ardent advocate of a shift away from Sino-Korean characters to pure *hangeul* in the process of modernization, Gale deeply lamented Koreans' diminished skill in Chinese character use following the abolition of the old state examinations in the mid-1890s. For Gale, the classical culture of China was an essential aspect of Korean cultural identity. It is hardly surprising, then, that Gale was delighted when he obtained *yadam* texts written by two ancient Korean scholars, Yi Ryuk and Im Bang.* He selected the stories he most admired, many of them about ghosts or supernatural events, others love stories or edifying tales of Confucian virtue, and published them as *Korean Folk Tales: Imps, Ghosts and Fairies* (London: J. M. Dent & Sons, 1913). Gale writes:

> An old manuscript copy of Im Bang's stories came into the hands of the translator a year ago, and he gives them now to the Western world that they may serve as introductory essays to the mysteries, and, what many call, absurdities of Asia. Very gruesome indeed, and

unlovely, some of them are, but they picture faithfully the conditions under which Im Bang himself, and many past generations of Koreans, have lived.

The thirteen short stories by Yi Ryuk are taken from a reprint of old Korean writings issued last year (1911), by a Japanese publishing company.

Part 1 of *Eerie Tales from Old Korea* includes stories from Hulbert's *Korea Review* Vol. 2–Vol. 5 (1902–1905), while Part 2 consists of stories from Gale's *Korean Folk Tales*. The present selection of ghost stories has been made because I believe they should be easily available to readers in the twenty-first century, precisely 100 years after the publication of Gale's volume. They are such fun to read! The literary style of the missionaries fits perfectly with the conventions of the ghost story in English. This collection does not aim to be anything more than a reprint of the texts published a century or more ago; the stories are mostly very simple and straightforward. They do not need lengthy footnotes. They can be read without difficulty, and many of them serve to remind us that ordinary Koreans were more than a match for almost any kind of ghost, spirit, or goblin, and often walked away with a mound of treasure or a beautiful wife in the bargain!

In 1900, Hulbert and Gale were among the main founders of the Royal Asiatic Society-Korea Branch. They were its two first speakers and their papers were the first two published in the first volume of RASKB's *Transactions*. And I am now president of the RASKB, a position that Gale held almost exactly a century ago. In addition, 2013 marks the 150th anniversary of their birth. What better reasons can there be to combine the ghostly tales published by these two great men for readers to enjoy today?

---

* Gale provides the following biographical information on the authors—which he took from *Gukjo Inmulji* (Korea's record of famous men)—in his original publication of *Korean Folk Tales*:

> Im Bang was born in 1640, the son of a provincial governor. He was very bright as a boy and from earliest years fond of study, becoming a great scholar. He matriculated first in his class in 1660, and graduated in 1663. He was a disciple of Song Si-yeol, one of Korea's first writers. In 1719, when he was in his eightieth year, he became governor of Seoul, and held as well the office of secretary of the Cabinet. In the year 1721 he got into difficulties over the choice of the Heir Apparent, and in 1722, on account of a part he played in a disturbance in the government, he was exiled to North Korea, where he died.

> Yi Ryuk lived in the reign of King Sejo, matriculated in 1459, and graduated first in his class in 1564. He was a man of many offices and many distinctions in the way of literary excellence.

Among many other writings, Yi Ryuk (李陸, 1438–1498) composed a collection of *yadam*, *Cheongpa-geukdam* (靑坡劇談). Im Bang (任埅, 1640–1724) was famed for his collection of *yadam*, *Cheonyerok* (天倪錄), from which these ghost stories are taken.

PART I

A Beggar's Wages

He was no beggar at first, nor need he ever have been one, but when the monk met him in front of his father's house and, pointing a bony finger at him, said, "You will be a beggar when you are fifteen years old!" it simply frightened him into being one. I've forgotten his name, but we can call him Palyungi, which name will do as well as any. He was twelve and the only son of wealthy parents. How the snuffling monk knew that he was going to be a beggar is more than I can say, but perhaps he envied the boy and his good prospects and was sharp enough to have learned that you can frighten some folks into doing most anything by just telling them that they are destined to do it.

Palyungi was a sensitive lad, and he never thought of doubting the monk's word. He reasoned that if he stayed at home and became a beggar, it would mean that his parents would also be reduced to want, while if he went away and became a sort of vicarious beggar, it might save them. How he induced his parents to let him go is not told, but one day he set out without a single coin in his pouch, not knowing whether he would ever see his father's home again. He wandered southward across the Hangang River through Chungcheong-do, across the lofty Joryeong (Bird Pass), begging his way from house to house. So sensitive was he that he hardly dared sleep under any man's roof for fear his evil fortune would be communicated to it. His clothes were in rags and he was growing thinner and thinner, eating sometimes of the chaff and beans that the horses left in the corners of their eating troughs, sometimes dining with the pigs.

At last, one night he was limping along the road toward a village when his courage gave out, and he sunk in a heap beside the road and gave up the struggle. He fell into a light, troubled sleep from which he was awakened by the sound of a galloping horse. It was now almost dark, but rising to his knees he saw a horse come pounding down the road with its halter trailing and no owner in sight. On the horse's back were two small but apparently heavy boxes. As the horse passed him he seized the trailing halter and speedily brought the animal to a standstill. These heavy boxes, what could they contain but money? For a moment the temptation was strong, but the next moment he gave a laugh as much as to say, "I'm not fifteen yet, what good would the money do me if I am to be a beggar anyway?" So he tied the horse to a tree out of sight of the road and walked along in the direction from which the horse had come.

He had not gone a mile when out of the darkness appeared a man evidently suffering from great excitement and running as fast as he could go. He fairly ran into Palyungi's arms. His first word was, "Have you seen my horse? I am undone if I cannot find him. He was loaded with the government tax from my district and if it is lost my head will be taken off and all my family reduced to poverty." The boy asked him the color of the horse and other particulars and, when sure that this was the owner of the horse he had caught, led him to the spot where he had tied it. The owner was so delighted that he fell to crying and, opening one of the boxes, took out a silver bar and tried to make the boy accept it, but he would not. After urging him in vain, the man went on his way with the horse and the treasure.

So Palyungi's wanderings continued for two years more. He slept under no man's roof for fear of bringing it evil fortune but made his bed in the stable or under a pile of straw or in any nook or corner he could find. At last, fortune led him to the village of Yangju late in the autumn when the frosts of winter were coming on. Someone invited him in to spend the night but he refused as usual, telling them that he might bring bad luck. As he turned away someone said, "There is a fine house up the valley among the hills and no one lives there. It is said to be haunted. Every person that lived there was killed by the *dokkaebis*. Why don't you go and stop there?" Palyungi thought it over. Here was a chance to sleep in a house without injuring anyone. He accepted the proposal and, after obtaining precise directions as to the position of the house, started out in great spirits. The *dokkaebis* surely would not have any interest in injuring him.

At last, among the trees, he spied the tile roof of a fine mansion. He entered the gate. All was silent. The open windows gaped at him. The silence was depressing, but Palyungi entered bravely. It was now nearly dark and everything was gloomy and indistinct, but the boy groped about till he found a cozy corner, and after munching a handful of boiled rice that he had brought in his sleeve rolled up in paper, he lay down and went to sleep, oblivious of ghosts and goblins. It might have been midnight or later when he started up, as wide awake as ever in his life. There was no apparent cause for this and yet he felt in the darkness about him an influence that was new to his experience. As he sat listening in the dark he heard a little rustling sound, and something soft and light brushed across his face like the wing of a butterfly.

This was too much. He was willing to meet the *dokkaebis* in the light but it was unfair to attack him in the dark. So he felt about in his pouch till he found his steel and tinder and struck a spark. This he applied to some little resinous splinters that he had brought for the purpose, and immediately a tiny flame sprang up. Holding this above his head, he peered about him into the darkness.

He was in a large room or hall and the beams and rafters above him were concealed by a paneled ceiling across which rainbow-colored dragons were chasing each other. Out toward the middle of the room he saw two long snake-like things hanging down from a hole in the ceiling. He shrank back in dismay, for this was worse than *dokkaebis*, but lighting some more of his sticks he soon perceived that these two things were not serpents but rope ends moving in the breeze. It was the frayed end of one of these that had brushed across his face in the dark. Now this was a very curious sight, and Palyungi was eager to learn what connection these ropes had with the tragedies that had been enacted in this house. So he boldly grasped one of the ropes and gave it a violent jerk. Down it came, accompanied by a clang like that of iron. On the end of it hung an enormous key.

Well, of course a key always suggests a money box, and a money box always suggests a miser, and misers in Korea are the special victims of *dokkaebis*, so putting two and two together Palyungi thought it would be worthwhile looking about a bit. Now, misers in Korea do not go and dig a hole in the ground to bury their money, perhaps because they are too lazy to dig it up every time they want to count it, but they often put it in a box and hide it among the beams above a ceiling. So Palyungi hunted about till he found an old ladder and then, crawling up through the hole in the ceiling, was rewarded by finding a small but very heavy box tucked away among the rafters. He gave it a push with his foot and sent it crashing down through the flimsy ceiling to the floor below. The key fitted, of course, and he found himself the possessor of a pile of silver bars, enough to make him enormously wealthy. There was at least four thousand dollars' worth—good wages for four years of begging! How would he ever be able to spend all that money?

It was now growing light and, shouldering his treasure trove, he trudged down the valley toward the village. Before he entered it, he hid his box under an overhanging bank. He then went into one of the houses and begged for something to eat at the kitchen door. The wench in charge bade him come in and warm his toes at the fire. It seemed that it was a feast day at that house, and as the boy sat there in the kitchen on the dirt floor he heard the host in the neighboring room telling his guests a remarkable adventure he had once had. He was carrying the government tax up to Seoul when his horse ran away, and all would have been lost had not a beggar boy caught the horse and restored it to him. Palyungi's ears pricked up at this. It sounded familiar. The man concluded by saying: "Ever since that I have been seeking for that boy, and I have laid aside for him one-third of all my income since that day, but I cannot find him." Palyungi, knowing that he would not now be dependent upon the man's bounty, opened the door of the room and made himself known. The gentleman clasped him in his arms and fell to crying, he was so glad. After a time, he told the boy that he had been provided for and should never need money again, but Palyungi smiled and said, "I shall not need your money for I have three times as much as your whole property is worth." He then led them to the place where he had hid the box and disclosed to their amazed eyes the treasure it contained. He was now sixteen years old and the prophecy had been fulfilled. So he went up to Seoul on his own donkey like a gentleman and found that his father and mother had suffered no calamity through him.

A Hunter's Mistake

He was a great hunter. If a cash piece were hung at a distance of ten paces he could put his arrow head into the hole in the cash without moving the coin. One day as he sat at his door, three geese flew by high in the air. One of the bystanders said, "You cannot bring down all those geese with one shot." He seized his bow and shot as the ancient mariner shot the albatross. The three geese came floundering to the ground.

That night the hunter dreamed that three fine boys came to him and said, "We are going to come and live at your house." Sure enough, that winter his wife presented him with boy triplets. He was inordinately proud of them. They grew up strong and handsome, but on their tenth birthday they all fell ill with smallpox and died a few days later at the same hour. The old man was inconsolable. He wrapped the bodies in straw and tied them, as is customary, to the branch of a tree on the mountainside to let the evil humors of the disease dry up before burying them, so that when buried the bodies would easily decay. Then in his grief he took to drink and would go about half drunk, bewailing his loss.

One night a crony of his in his tipsy ramblings stumbled along the mountainside and fell asleep right under where these three bodies hung tied to the tree. Late at night he awoke, and the moon shone down upon him between the bodies. It was a gruesome sight. Just then the sound of a wailing cry came up from the village below where the sorrow-stricken father, staggering homeward, gave vent to his grief. The man listened. A murmuring sound came from overhead. Was one of the corpses speaking?

"Listen! Brothers, we have our revenge on the wicked hunter. Hear his wailing cry. His life is wrecked. As we flew through the sky, three happy geese, he laid us low at one wanton stroke, but now we are even with him. Sleep quietly, brothers, our work is done."

The next day when the hunter heard of this he broke his good bow across his knee and never shot another arrow.

THE DONKEY MAKER

When he was a young man, the celebrated Jeong Mong-ju, the last of the Goryeo statesmen, went up to the capital to attend the national examinations but did not succeed in passing. On his way home in company with six young fellow travelers, he entered the outskirts of Majun in Gyeonggi-do. They were all very hungry, and seeing an old woman sitting beside the road selling bean-bread, they eagerly purchased a piece to stay their hunger till they should reach their inn and get a good meal.

Jeong Mong-ju never did things in a hurry. He always preferred to wait and see how things turned out before experimenting. He noticed that the old woman did not give them the bread that was in the tray before her but reached around and produced another batch of bread from which she cut generous portions and gave to his companions. They ate it with great gusto, but before they had finished they began to act very curiously, wagging their heads and acting altogether like crazy men.

Jeong saw that something was wrong. He suspected that the bread had been medicated in some way. Looking intently at the old woman, he perceived that her face wore a very curious, inhuman look. Going close to her, he said, "You must eat a piece of this bread yourself or I shall strike you dead on the spot." There was no escape and Jeong evidently meant what he said, so she had to take a piece and eat it. The effect was the same as on his companions. She began to go wild like them.

Turning he was amazed to find that his six fellow travelers had all turned into donkeys. He leaped toward the driveling old woman and said fiercely, "Tell me the antidote instantly or I will throttle you." The old woman had just enough sense left to point to the other bread and say, "That will cure them," before she, too, was transformed into a donkey. Jeong put a straw rope through her mouth, mounted her, and drove her furiously up the hill, lashing the donkey with all his might. It did not take long to tire her out. When she was exhausted, Jeong dismounted and, facing the animal, said, "I charge you to assume your original and proper shape."

The poor broken donkey began to wag her head

this way and that and soon her form began to change to that of a white fox. Before the transformation was complete Jeong seized a club and with one blow crushed the animal's skull. This done, he hurried back to his six unfortunate companions and fed them the bread that the old woman had said was the antidote. A few minutes later they had all turned back into men.

That night these six young men all dreamed the same thing, namely, that an old man met Jeong Mong-ju on the road and charged him with having killed his wife, striking him on the head so that the blood flowed down on his shoulder. In the morning, strange to relate, it was found that there was a wound on the young man's temple. The dreams proved prophetic, for when at last Jeong Mong-ju met his death at the hand of an assassin on Seonjuk Bridge in Songdo, the blow that felled him was delivered on that very spot on his head.

A Submarine Adventure

Haeinsa, the Monastery of the Ocean Seal, is one of the most important centers of Buddhism in Korea. It is in the town of Hapcheon and counts its monastics by the hundreds. Its archives are piled with wood blocks cut with Sanskrit characters, and the whole place is redolent with the odor of Buddhist sanctity. But it is the name which piques our curiosity and demands an explanation. The Ocean Seal does not refer to the marine animal whose pelt forms an article of commerce but rather the seal with which a legal document is stamped. The genesis of this name may appear fanciful to the matter-of-fact Western mind, but we can assure the reader that it is the most rational explanation he will find, and we would remind him at the same time that there are more things in heaven and earth than are dreamt of in any Western system of philosophy.

Hong Song-won was one of those literary flowers that are born to blush unseen and waste their sweetness on the desert air of central Korea. Virtue is its own reward, but that reward seldom takes the form of bread and butter, so while Hong was virtuous he was lamentably poor. His literary attainments forbade his earning his living by the sweat of his brow so he earned it by the sweat of his slave's brow, who went about begging food from the neighbors. Curiously enough, this did not sully his honor as work would have done.

As he was sitting one day in his room meditating upon the partiality of fortune, a strange dog came running into the yard and curled up in a corner as if this had always been its home. It attached itself to Hong and accompanied him wherever he went. Hong took a great liking to the animal and would share with it even his scanty bowl of rice, much to the disgust of the faithful slave by whose efforts alone the food had been obtained. One morning the dog began wagging its tail and jumping about as if begging its master to take a walk. Hong complied and the dog led straight toward the river. It ran into the water and then came back and seemed to invite its master to mount its back and ride into the stream. Hong drew the line at such a prank, but when he saw the dog dash into the water and cross with incredible speed, he caught the spirit of the occasion and so far curtailed his *yangban* dignity as to seat himself on the dog's back.

To his consternation, the dog sank with him to the bottom of the river, but as he found no difficulty in breathing and naturally felt some delicacy about trusting himself alone to the novel element, he held fast to the dog and was rewarded shortly by a sight of the palace of His Majesty the Dragon King of the Deep. Dismounting at the door, he joined the crowd of tortoises and octopi and other courtiers of the deep who were seeking an audience with their dread sovereign. No one challenged his entrance, and soon he stood in his presence. The king greeted him cordially and asked him why he had delayed so long in coming. Hong carried on the polite fiction by answering that he had been very delinquent in paying his respects so late but that several kinds of important business had prevented his coming sooner.

The upshot of the matter was that the sea king made him tutor to the crown prince, who studied his characters with such assiduity that in six months his education was complete. By this time Hong was beginning to long for a breath of fresh air and made bold to intimate as much to His Majesty, who made no objection but insisted upon loading him down with gifts. The crown prince drew him aside and whispered, "If he asks you to name the thing you would like best as a reminder of your stay with us, don't fail to name that wooden seal on the table over yonder."

It was an ordinary-looking thing and Hong wondered of what use it could be to him, but he had seen too many queer things to be skeptical, so when the king asked him what he would like he asked only for the wooden seal. The king not only gave him the seal but the more costly gifts as well. With his capacious sleeve full of pink coral mixed with lustrous pearls and with the seal in his hand, he mounted the dog and sped away homeward. A short half hour sufficed to land him on the bank of the stream where he had entered, and with the dog at his heels he wended his way across the fields toward his former home.

When he arrived at the spot where his little thatched hut should be standing, he found the site occupied by a beautiful and capacious building. Had he indeed lost the only place he could call home? Anxiously he entered the place and inquired for the owner. The young man who seemed to be in charge answered gravely that some twenty years before, the owner had wandered away with his dog and never returned. "And who then are you?" asked the astonished Hong. "I am his son." Hong gazed at him critically and, sure enough, the young man looked just as his son would have looked. He made himself known and great was the rejoicing in that house. There were a thousand questions to be asked and answered: "And where did this fine house come from?" "Why, you see, the dog that you went away with came back regularly every month, bringing in his mouth a bar of gold and then disappearing again. We soon had enough to build this place and buy all the surrounding rice fields." "And it has been twenty years! I thought only six months had passed. They evidently live very fast down there under the sea."

Hong found no difficulty in adapting himself to the new situation. He was well on in years now but was very well preserved, as one might expect from his having been in brine for the last twenty years. But he found no use for the seal that he had brought. After several months had passed, a monk came wandering by and stopped to talk with the old gentleman. In the course of the conversation, it transpired that Hong had visited the sea king's domain. The monk asked eagerly, "And did you see the wonderful seal?" "See it?" said Hong, "I not only saw it but I brought it back with me." The monk trembled with excitement. "Bring it here," he begged. Hong brought out the seal and placed it in the hands of the holy man.

The monk took a piece of paper and wrote on it: "Ten ounces of gold." Then, without inking the seal, he pressed it on the paper and lo! it left a bright red impress without even being wet. This done, the monk folded the paper and, setting fire to it, tossed it into the air. It burned as it fell, and at the point where the charred remnants touched the ground was seen a bright bar of gold of ten ounces weight. This then was the secret. No matter what sum was asked for, the impress of that seal would surely bring it.

They kept it going pretty constantly for the next few days, as you may easily imagine. The monk received an enormous sum, with which he built the magnificent monastery and named it appropriately Haeinsa, or the Ocean Seal Monastery. He went all the way to India to bring the sacred Sanskrit books and the wood blocks were cut and piled in the library of the monastery. Beneath them was hidden the marvelous seal, but Koreans say that during the last Japan-China war* it disappeared. The man who holds it is probably ignorant of its value. If his eye happens to fall upon this and he discovers the virtues of the seal, we trust he will do the proper thing, as Hong did by the monk who showed him its secret.

---

* Possibly in reference to the First Sino-Japanese War (1894–1895).

NECESSITY,
THE MOTHER OF INVENTION

Han Chun-deuk was without doubt a very wealthy man, even from a Western standpoint. His annual income consisted of 200,000 bags of rice. He lived just above the Supyodari (Water Gauge Bridge), a fashionable quarter of the city in those days—namely, a hundred and fifty years ago. But he was as generous as he was rich. Fifty thousand bags of rice were consumed yearly in supporting his near and distant relatives and fifty thousand more in charities, or we might better say, in other charities. Anyone who was ill or in distress or lacked the means to bury a parent or take a wife had but to appeal to Mr. Han and the means would be forthcoming. In such veneration was this philanthropist held by the whole community that never was anything, not even a tile, stolen from his place.

Such was the man whom one Jo, living in Nugakgol west of Gyeongbokgung Palace, marked for his victim. This Jo had come of a wealthy family but his elder brother, who of course took charge of the estate upon the demise of the father, had squandered the patrimony in riotous living and, dying childless, left Jo a legacy of debts. These had eaten up the remnants of the estate and now, thrown upon a cold and heartless world, the man—accustomed to a life of ease and uninstructed in any useful trade—was in danger of falling to the status of "poor white trash," as that term is applied in certain portions of America. His wife stood in the imminent, deadly breach and fought back the enemy by making tobacco pouches, which she put on the market at ten cash apiece.

One day Jo came in and sat for an hour in deep thought, paying no attention to any words that were addressed to him, but finally raised his head and exclaimed: "I have it." His wife gave him a quick startled glance followed by a doubtful sort of smile which seemed to say, "Yes, you seem to have it very bad," but she did not say it aloud. "Within two days we will be wealthy folks again," he said. His reason was evidently tottering. "Hm! The price of tobacco pouches must have gone way up then," she said. He gave her a glance of scorn. "Give me one hundred cash and I will build up a fortune as if by magic," he cried. "This is no experiment. It's a sure thing."

She heaved a sigh as if she had heard of sure things before, but nevertheless produced the hundred cash. With this small amount of capital he went to work and made good his word, for ere twenty-four hours had passed he was enormously wealthy. And this moving tale hangs upon the means which he employed to amass a fortune in so short a space of time.

Taking his hundred cash, he left the house and was gone all the afternoon. In the evening he returned and spent the major portion of the night in putting a razor edge on a small knife that he had purchased. His wife wondered whether he were going into the barber business or to cut his own throat, but she asked no questions. The following morning, at a proper hour, Jo presented himself at the gate of the wealthy Han Chun-deuk and asked to see the master of the house. As Jo was a stranger, the gateman of course replied that his master was out, but as Jo was insistent he affected an entrance and, having announced his approach to the rich man's reception room by clearing his throat vigorously, he bowed himself into the presence of the philanthropist.

It was still too early for the usual callers to be present, and the two men had the room to themselves. After a few irrelevant remarks on the weather and the latest news, the caller came to the point. "Ahem! I have a very special word to speak to you this morning. The fact is that though formerly in good circumstances, I have become reduced to the greatest poverty and am in great need of a thousand ounces of silver with which to engage in business. Could you kindly let me have it?" A thousand ounces of silver! It took even Han's breath away. A thousand ounces of silver! Well, well, here was a case. The history of his philanthropies had seen no such monumental effrontery. And he an unknown man, asking for a thousand ounces of silver before he had told his name or been in the room ten minutes.

The good man fairly stammered, "But, but—how—but how can I give you all that silver when I don't know you or anything about your particular circumstances, or your plans?" The visitor sat with downcast eyes and never a sign of embarrassment on his features. He spoke in a slow unimpassioned voice. "It simply means that unless you give me the silver, my life ends today," and he fixed the poor philanthropist with a glassy stare that made him shiver. "Why, my dear fellow, how in the world—what is the sense—I don't see where the logic of it comes in. Here you come, a perfect stranger, and . . ."

"That has nothing to do with it at all, I need a thousand ounces of silver or my life is forfeit." "But a thousand ounces! Come now; let us say a hundred and I will let you have it, but a thousand—no, no." "Very well," answered Jo in the same quiet tone, and he rose as if to go but as he gained his feet he drew out the sharp knife, plunged it into his own abdomen, and cut a frightful gash from left to right; he fell headlong before the horrified Han and lay weltering in his own lifeblood. The poor philanthropist wrung his hands in an agony of fear. What should he do? The knife had fallen to the floor at his feet, and who would believe that the unknown visitor had killed himself? He sprang to the outer door and made it fast. Then he went to the inner apartments and sent one of the woman slaves to call his trusted body servant. Him only he admitted into the presence of the dead and told the story, and begged the servant to help him out of the difficulty. The latter thought a few moments and then said. "What is the man's name and where does he live?" "He never told his name but from what he said I judge that his home is in Nugakgol." "Well, then the only thing to do is to let me put the body in a straw bag together with the knife and carry it to Nugakgol, set it down there somewhere, and then under pretense of going for a drink of wine I can slip away. The bag will be opened and the people there will recognize the dead man and take him to his home." "Just the thing!" cried the master, and a great load seemed lifted off his mind, but while the servant was away finding the bag, the fear came back, not the fear of detection but fear lest the spirit of the dead should bring him evil.

This impression grew stronger and stronger. How

could this calamity be averted? Perhaps if he complied with the dead man's request it would quiet the departed spirit. So he brought from his strongbox a thousand ounces of silver, about sixty pounds in weight, and tied them securely in one corner of the skirt of the dead man's coat. But he did not tell his servant this, for even the most faithful of servants might think the silver better spent upon the living than upon the dead. When the servant returned, the body, just as it was, was unceremoniously dumped into the straw bag and placed upon a *jige*, a porter's carrying frame. The servant found the load heavier than he had anticipated but finally arrived in Nugakgol. It was just noon of a sultry summer day and the streets were nearly deserted. He set down his burden in a returned corner and wiped the perspiration from his brow.

He glanced around the corner and saw that the coast was clear, so, hastily throwing the bag upon the ground, he shouldered the *jige* and made off; but some evil chance made him turn back to see if the bag was all right. Oh horror of horrors! A ghastly face was peering at him over the edge of the bag. One eye was winking violently while the other was concealed by the headband that had become displaced. The mouth was screwed into a shape that put to shame the devil guardians of the realms of hell, such as he had seen depicted in the monasteries. With a low moan of terror he started back, but just at that point a ditch crossed the street and, stepping into this, he was sent sprawling on the ground. Another instant and he was up and off at a pace that would bid defiance to the fleetest *dokkaebi* that ever dogged the footsteps of mortal man.

The face above the edge of the bag watched the stricken fugitive out of sight and then a broad smile took the place of the diabolical grimace that had done its work so well. Jo, for it was none other, emerged from the bag and, as bedraggled, ensanguined, and disheveled as he was, hugged that heavy coat skirt in his arms and slunk into a neighboring doorway, for chance had favored him and he had been put down almost before his own house. Before many days had elapsed, Jo and his family moved to the south, where he invested in piece goods and other products of sunny Jeolla-do.

Three years went by, each one of which doubled the capital of the thrifty Jo, and again we see him in Seoul, dressed in the best the silk shops could offer and standing once more before the gate of the great Han Chun-deuk. No one challenged him this time. His gorgeous raiment was passport enough. He found the philanthropist in his reception room and, after introducing himself, came right down to business. "Didn't you lend a man a thousand ounces of silver some three years ago?" Great heavens! the murder was out. This man might have the police at his back. He must be "fixed," and that immediately.

"Hush," whispered the poor philanthropist, "not quite so loud please. So you know about that little thing, too. Well, I can make it better worth your while to keep still about it than to bring it to the notice of the authorities." "On the other hand," replied the visitor calmly, "I am here on purpose to pay back that loan." "You?" "Yes, you see, I am the man whom you sent away in the bag." Han was speechless. "Yes, I want both to pay back the money and make a confession. It was a desperate chance with me. I was driven quite to the wall, and if it had not been for that pig's bladder full of beef blood that I carried under my coat, I don't know how in the world I could have brought about a change in my fortunes. But I am well off now and am ready to pay back the silver with interest." And he told the wondering Han about his business venture. It was fully ten minutes before Han had fairly gotten his breath again, and then he exclaimed: "By the shades of Yi Sun-sin, that was the neatest thing I ever heard of! I won't take back a cent of that money; you earned it all and more. But, I say, come up to Seoul and I can put you onto something much better than piece goods. I want someone to help me handle my property and teach my son to carry on the estate. You are just the man. Say you'll come." And Jo came.

THE ESSENCE OF LIFE

It may not be generally known to zoologists and natural historians that if a fox lives five hundred years, its life essence condenses or crystallizes into a jewel and lies in the mouth of the animal. Neither would Yu Seong-ryong have known it had it not been for a fortunate conjunction of circumstances. He was a young man of twenty and unmarried, and he lived in the southern town of Andong.

One day as he sat at study, he looked up and saw a most beautiful woman pass by. He was simply fascinated and could not but follow her. This was very bad form, indeed, but he was hardly accountable for his actions. The next day, his old teacher looked at him sharply and upbraided him, and the young man confessed his fault but pleaded as his excuse that he had been virtually hypnotized. He told the old man that every time the woman opened her mouth to speak, something like a diamond flashed between her teeth. The old man gave a violent start and exclaimed: "The next time you see her, get possession of that jewel and swallow it instantly in spite of her tears." A few days after, the fair vision passed his window again, and as before, he felt the mesmeric attraction, but he followed this time with a fixed purpose. He overtook the woman and entered into conversation with her, during the course of which he said, "What is that beautiful jewel that I see in your mouth?" "Ah, I mustn't tell you that," she answered. He pretended to be much offended. "Let me see it—just once," he said.

She took it from her month and held it up between her thumb and finger. The ungallant Yu snatched it from her and swallowed it in a trice. The woman uttered a piercing scream and fell to the ground, writhing as if in agony and weeping in a most heartrending way. Yu was almost sorry for what he had done, but when he saw the form of the woman begin to assume the shape of a white fox, his pity was changed to exultation. The fox slunk away up hill and Yu went home.

He had swallowed the Essence of life, and from that day on he had but to read a book once to master it. One glance at a page and he could repeat every word by heart. After passing before a line of ten thousand men he could tell, the next time he passed, whether the position of any one of them had been changed. It hardly need be said that he became the most famous scholar in the land. But he had no wife, and it was high time that his bachelor days should be finished.

One day as he was on his way to Seoul, he stopped at an inn by the Hangang River. The innkeeper was a gentleman in reduced circumstances, and that night his young and clever daughter dreamt that she saw a dragon climbing a willow. In the morning she saw through a hole in the window the young man Yu standing in the yard. She was much taken with his appearance and so far set aside the dictates of modesty as to ask her father what his name was. "His name is Yu Seong-ryong, I believe." "Is it possible?" she cried. "Why that means, 'Willow becomes dragon!'" Then she told her dream. The father saw the point and approached the young man with a proposition that needed no urging after he had once accidentally caught a glimpse of the girl's face. And the wedding came off all in good time.

The Goose That Laid the Golden Egg

His name was Lee, which by interpretation means Plum Tree. Now Mr. Plum Tree was a Korean of a nomadic turn of mind. He spent his time wandering about the country, seeing the sights and enjoying himself generally. He was not encumbered with superfluous wealth but had enough to keep him on the road. Having traveled over all the eight provinces,* he crossed the border into China and worked his way south till he approached Nanking, then the capital of China.

---

* Refers to the eight provinces of Korea during the Joseon Dynasty: Chungcheong-do, Gangwon-do, Gyeonggi-do, Gyeongsang-do, Hamgyeong-do, Hwanghae-do, Jeolla-do, and Pyeongan-do.

One afternoon as he was approaching a village, he saw a magpie seated on the crossbeam of a gateway, but on coming near he found that if was only a painting of a magpie, but done so skillfully as to deceive the eye at a little distance. Wondering who the artist could be, he called out to the gateman but instead a girl came out and asked what he wanted. The girl was the most beautiful he had ever met. He asked who the artist might be and she said, "I painted the magpie. You see, I am an orphan and have not enough money to pay the funeral expenses of my mother. So I painted the magpie hoping that someone might come along to whom I would sell myself as a slave for a single day and thus gain the necessary money to bury my mother."

Young Plum Tree was a good-hearted fellow and pitied the girl so much that he then and there put in her hands all the money he had about him and told her to go into business and earn enough to bury her mother. Her gratitude exceeded all bounds, for he had saved her from an awful fate. She took the money and Plum Tree went on his way as a beggar. A year later as he was wandering about the streets of Nanking, he met this same girl and she gladly told him that she had succeeded and would like to reward him, but the only thing she had was a screen on which was a magpie that she had embroidered. She told him to carry it home, put it in a closet, and look at it *only once a day*. He wondered at this injunction but obeyed.

Reaching home at last, he put the embroidery away and would have forgotten all about it had not poverty driven him to think of pawning it. When he opened the box in which it lay, he was astonished to see a little bar of silver drop from the beak of the embroidered bird. Was ever such a thing seen before! He took the money and bought rice and wood. The next day he looked again, and another bar of silver rewarded him. And so it went on, day after day, until he was a very wealthy man.

At last the time came for him to die and, calling his son, he told him the secret and charged him to look at the bird only once a day. The boy promised to obey, but after the three years of mourning were over, he became a spendthrift and, forgetting his father's words, began to take a peep at the bird two or three times a day. This made him reckless, and one day he kept looking every few minutes all day long, and each time was rewarded by a silver bar. But the next day when he opened the box, the bird looked tired and sick, and instead of silver, tears dropped.

The young man then remembered his father's words and was struck with remorse. That night a beautiful young girl came in his dreams and chided him for his folly, saying his good fortune had flown. And so it proved, for when he went to see the bird the next day it was gone, and the silk panel on which it was embroidered was a blank. So Plum Tree Jr. died of starvation.

AN AESCULAPIAN EPISODE

He was only five years old when his father died and left him heir to a large property, and by the time he was twelve his relatives had succeeded in absorbing the whole estate. Cast upon his own resources, he wandered away in search of something to do to keep body and soul together. In course of time he came to the great salt works at Ulsan and hired himself out to one of the foremen there. Down beside the sea, about on a level with the tidewater, were scores of little thatched hovels. In each of them was a huge vat for holding salt water, with a fireplace beneath. Across the top of the vats heavy ropes were hung, and these, being dipped frequently in the boiling brine, became covered with crystals of salt, which were removed and sent to market. In one of these hovels our hero, Je-gal, was employed in bringing up sea water in buckets and feeding the fires. It was not long before his only suit of clothes became so saturated with salt that they formed a true barometer; for, as salt attracts moisture, he could tell whenever it was going to rain by the dampness of his clothes. When it was dry, his clothes were always stiff with the dry salt.

One bright morning when everyone was putting out his rice in the sun to dry, Je-gal begged his master not to do so, as it was sure to rain. His master laughed at him but complied, and in a short time a heavy rain came on that wet the other people's rice and caused a heavy loss. His master was astonished and asked Je-gal how he knew it was going to rain, but the boy kept his secret. In time, everybody in that district found it well to wait for Je-gal's master to act before they would sow or reap their crops or put out their damp rice to dry. The boy's reputation spread throughout all the countryside and he was looked upon as a genuine prophet.

One day news came that the king had been attacked by a very mysterious malady that none of the court physicians could cure. Everything was done for him that human skill could do but still he sank. At last royal messengers came to Ulsan saying that the king had heard of Je-gal and wanted him to come up to Seoul and prescribe for him. The boy protested that he could do nothing, but they urged and commanded until he could do nothing but comply. When the road to Seoul had been half covered and the way led up the steeps of Bird Pass, three brothers intercepted the party and begged that the boy Je-gal turn aside to their house among the hills and prescribe for their mother, who was at the point of death. The royal attendants protested, but the three brothers carried sharper arguments than words, so the whole party turned aside and followed the brothers to their house, a magnificent building hidden among the hills.

What was Je-gal to do? He did not know the use of a single drug. To gain time he said that he could do nothing for the patient till the following morning. In the middle of the night he heard a voice outside the gate calling softly, "O, Mr. Hinge, Mr. Hinge." A voice from within replied and the visitors asked eagerly, "Can't we come in now?" The person addressed as Mr. Hinge replied in the negative and the visitors reluctantly departed. Now who could Mr. Hinge be? Je-gal had never heard such a queer name before, so he investigated. Going to the gate he called, "Mr. Hinge, Mr. Hinge." "Well, what do you want?" came from one of the iron hinges of the door. "Who was it that just called?" asked the boy. "To tell the truth," answered the hinge, "the visitors were three white foxes masquerading as men. They have bewitched the old lady who is sick and came to kill her, but I would not let them in." "But you surely are not in league with these rogues. Tell me how I can save the old lady from them."

The Hinge complied and gave the boy explicit directions on how to act upon the morrow, and at dawn the three brothers came to take his orders. He commanded that three large kettles of oil should be heated hot and that six men with three saws and six pairs of tongs should be secured. These things having been done, he led the way down the path till he reached three aged oak trees standing by themselves. These he had the men saw off six feet from the ground. They all proved to be hollow. Then two men stood upon each stump and, reaching down with the tongs, lifted the kettles of hot oil and poured it down the hollow stumps. Two of the white foxes were scalded to death but the third one with nine tails leaped out and made its escape.

When the party got back to the house, the old lady appeared to be *in articulo mortis*, but a good dose of ginseng tea brought her around and in an hour she was perfectly well. The three brothers, and in fact the whole party, including the royal attendants, were amazed and delighted with this exhibition of medical skill, and the brothers urged him to name his fee. He replied that the only thing he wanted was a certain old rusty hinge on one of the doors beside the gate. They expostulated with him but he firmly refused any other reward. The hinge was drawn out, and with this strange talisman safely in his pouch Je-gal fared gaily toward the capital, feeling sure that he held the key to the situation.

Late one afternoon he was ushered into the presence of his royal patient. He felt his pulse and examined the symptoms in a knowing way and then said that the next morning he would prescribe. At dead of night he took out the hinge and held a long consultation with it, the result of which was that in the morning he ordered six kettles of hot oil and five men with a *garae*, or "power-shovel," as it might be called. Leading the way to a secluded spot behind the king's private apartments, he ordered the men to dig at a certain point. Half an hour's work revealed a hole about eight inches in diameter. The oil was poured down this hole, and to the consternation of all the witnesses, the earth began to heave and fall above the spot and there emerged, struggling in his death agonies, an angleworm eight feet long and eight inches thick. When this loathsome object expired, they all hurried in to the king, who seemed to be breathing his last, but a good drink of ginseng soup brought him round again and he was entirely recovered.

Je-gal said that the symptoms plainly pointed toward angleworm enchantment due to the fact that the worm had tasted of the king's bathwater. Honors were heaped upon the young "physician," and he became the pet of the court. This might have finished his medical career had not news come from China that the Empress was the victim of some occult disease which defied the leeches of Peking, and the King of Korea was ordered to send his most distinguished physician to the Chinese court. Of course, Dr. Je-gal was the one to go.

The rich cavalcade crossed the Yalu River and was halfway across Manchuria when Je-gal felt the hinge stirring in his pouch. He took it out and had a consultation with it, in the course of which the hinge said: "When you come to the next parting in the road, make your whole company take the right hand road and take the left yourself, alone. Before you have gone far you will come to a little hut—call for a cup of wine. The old man in charge will offer you three bowls of a most offensive liquor, but you must drink them down without hesitation and then ask as your reward his dog and his falcon."

The young man followed these queer directions, but when the old man offered him the three bowls he found them filled with a whitish liquid streaked with blood. He knew the hinge must be obeyed, however, and so he gulped down the horrible mixture without stopping to think. No sooner was it down than the old man overwhelmed him with thanks and called him all sorts of good names. It appeared that the old man had been a spirit in heaven but for some fault had been banished to earth and ordered to stay there till he could find someone to drink those three bowls of nauseating liquid.

He had been waiting two hundred years for the chance that had now come and released him from his bondage.

He offered Je-gal any gift he might wish, but the young man refused everything except the dog and the falcon. These the old man readily gave, and with dog at heel and bird on wrist, the young practitioner fared on, meeting his cavalcade a few miles further along the road. At last the gates of Peking loomed up in the distance, and the young physician was led into the Forbidden City by a brilliant escort. It was dusk as he entered, and he was taken first to his apartment for some refreshment. Meanwhile, the ailing Empress was suffering from intense excitement and demanding with screaming insistence that the physician from Korea should not be allowed to enter the palace but should be executed at once. Of course, this was considered the raving of a disordered mind and was not listened to.

The Empress declared that the Korean doctor should not come near her, but the following morning he was escorted to her apartment, where he was separated from her only by a screen. Je-gal declared that if a string were tied about her wrist and passed through a hole in the screen, he could diagnose the case by holding the other end. It was done, but the Empress, who seemed to be in the very extreme of terror, fought against it with all her might. Je-gal held the string a moment as if some telepathic power were passing from the patient to himself, but only for a moment. Dropping the string, he gave the screen a push, which sent it crashing to the floor, and at the same instant he rolled out from one of his flowing sleeves the little dog and from the other the hawk. The former flew at the Empress' throat and the latter at her eyes while the Emperor, who stood by, was struck dumb with amazement at this sort of treatment.

A sort of free fight followed in which Emperors, Empresses, dogs, and falcons were indiscriminately mixed, but the animals conquered and the Empress lay dead before them. The Emperor denounced Je-gal as a murderer, but he stood perfectly still with folded arms and said only, "Watch the body." The Emperor turned to the corpse and to his horror saw it slowly change its form to that of an enormous white fox with nine tails. Then he knew the truth—that his Empress had been destroyed and this beast had assumed her shape. "But where then is the Empress gone?" he cried. "Take up the boards of the floor and see," the young man replied. It was done and there they found the bones of the unfortunate Empress, who had been devoured by the fox.

Deep as was the Emperor's grief, he knew that a heavy load had been lifted from the Middle Kingdom, and he sent Je-gal back home loaded with honors and wealth. As he came to the Yalu River he felt the hinge moving in his pouch and took it out. The rusty bit of iron said, "Let me have a look at this beautiful river." Je-gal held it up with thumb and finger over the swift current of the stream, and with one leap it wrenched itself from his hand and sank in the water. At the same moment a sort of mist came before Je-gal's eyes, and from that hour he was blind. For a time he could not guess the enigma, but at last it came to him. The hinge's work was done and it must go back to its own, but in order that Je-gal might not be called upon to exercise the physician's office again he was made blind. So back to Seoul he went, where he lived till old age, an object of reverence to all the court and all the common people of Korea.

CATS AND THE DEAD

About two centuries and a half ago, a boy, who later became the great scholar Sa Jae, went to bed one night after a hard day's work on his Chinese. He had not been asleep long when he awoke with a start. The moon was shining in at the window and dimly lighting the room. Something was moving just outside the door. He lay still and listened. The door swung of its own accord and a tall black object came gliding into the room and silently took its place in the corner. The boy mastered his fear and continued gazing into the darkness at his ominous visitor. He was a very strong-minded lad and after a while, seeing that the black ghost made no movement, he turned over and went to sleep.

The moment he awoke in the morning, he turned his eyes to the corner and there stood his visitor still. It was a great black coffin standing on end with the lid nailed on and evidently containing its intended occupant. The boy gazed at it a long while and at last a look of relief came over his face. He called in his servant and said, "Go down to the village and find out who has lost a corpse."

Soon the servant came running back with the news that the whole village was in an uproar. A funeral had been in progress but the watchers by the coffin had fallen asleep, and when they awoke coffin and corpse had disappeared. "Go and tell the chief mourner to come here." When that excited individual appeared, the boy called him into the room and, pointing to the corner, said quietly, "What is that?" The hemp-clad mourner gazed in wonder and consternation. "That? That's my father's coffin. What have you been doing? You've stolen my father's body and disgraced me forever." The boy smiled and said, "How could I bring it here? It came of its own accord. I awoke in the night and saw it enter."

The mourner was incredulous and angry. "Now I will tell you why it came here," said the boy. "You have a cat in your house and it must be that it jumped over the coffin. This was such an offense to the dead that by some occult power, coffin, corpse, and all came here to be safe from further insult. If you don't believe it, send for your cat and we will see." The challenge was too direct to refuse, and a servant was sent for the cat. Meanwhile, the mourner tried to lay the coffin down on its side, but, with all his strength, he could not budge it an inch. The boy came up to it and gave it three strokes with his hand on the left side and a gentle push. The dead recognized the master hand, and the coffin was easily laid on its side.

When the cat arrived and was placed in the room, the coffin, of its own accord, rose on its end again, a position in which it was impossible for the cat to jump over it. The wondering mourner accepted the explanation, and that day the corpse was laid safely in the ground. But to this day, the watchers beside the dead are particularly careful to see that no cat enters the mortuary chamber lest it disturb the peace of the deceased.

A KOREAN JONAH

He was on his way to China on a junk, from the harbor of Pungdeok, in company with a considerable company of merchants. All went well until they neared the vicinity of certain islands in the Yellow Sea. At this point the water became horribly agitated and a most violent storm lay upon them. At last they came to the conclusion that the spirits were angry at one of their number, so they cast lots, and the lot fell upon our friend Jo, who, so far as he remembered, had no quarrel with the spirits. They were about to throw him into the sea when one of their number, more compassionate than the rest, suggested that they try to land him on an island that they could see through the driving spray. They managed to find a sheltered nook in which they took refuge from the storm, and as soon as they were able they landed Jo, together with sundry bags of grain.

The moment he set foot on dry ground, the storm ceased as if by magic, and the merchants went on their way rejoicing. Our friend Jo was now, by force of circumstances, turned from a Jonah into a Robinson Crusoe. He built himself a hut in a crevice of the rocks and kept a sharp lookout for boats sailing Koreaward, but none appeared. He noticed that every four days, the sea would become terribly agitated for a few hours and then suddenly stop. One day as he sat on a point of rocks, watching the distant horizon for a sail, he learned the cause of the periodical disturbances, for a gigantic sea serpent lifted its head from the waves and came rolling toward the shore. Its coming was accompanied by a howling gale, and the sea was lashed into a fury. Gaining the shore, the serpent crawled into a hole in the rocks.

Jo, having played Jonah and Robinson Crusoe, now began to play St. George, for he seemed to know in some occult way that his own salvation depended on his killing the dragon. He studied the habits of the reptile and found that it never stirred out of its hole for two days and that it always slid down a certain grooved path into the sea. He bound a sharp knife to the end of a stake and planted it in the middle of the serpent's path with the keen edge pointing toward the hole. He then lay down behind a rock and watched from afar. The serpent came out and glided down its accustomed path; the knife pierced its throat. According to snake nature, the reptile would not retreat but thought to gain the sea and so be safe. It therefore passed over the knife so that its entire body was slit open from end to end.

Its contortions were so terrible that Jo fled in dismay and dared not return until a horrible stench apprised him of the fact that the serpent was surely dead. Then he came and found that the ground all about the body was covered ankle deep with gems, with which, as everybody knows, a dragon's insides are always lined. Jo thereupon shifted the scene again from St. George to Sinbad the Sailor and filled his now empty rice bags with priceless gems. Not long after, he saw the returning sails of his friends, who were on their way back to Korea and stopped to pick him up. When they saw his bags and asked what they contained, he gave an idiotic grin and said they were full of nice gobang* stones that he had been making during his leisure hours. They thought that solitude had driven him mad, so they took him and his heavy bags back to Korea, where he became the wealthiest man in all the realm.

_____

* A variant on the classic Asian strategy game go. It is also called gomoku.

A Brave Governor

Once upon a time, a newly appointed governor of Gyeongsang-do went to his post in Daegu but suddenly died within four days. Another was sent and he followed the bad example of the first. A third was sent, but news came back that he, too, died in the same mysterious manner. Now the governorship of that province is generally considered a pretty good thing, but after three governors had died in succession there was a visible falling off in applicants for the position. In fact, no one could be found who would venture. The king was quite uneasy over the situation but had no way of finding out where the difficulty lay. Not even the *ajeons** of Daegu could give any reason for it. In every case the governor had been found dead in his bed the third morning after his arrival.

At this juncture one of the officials of *seungji* rank proposed to His Majesty that he should be sent as governor and boldly offered his services. The king was much moved by the man's offer to go but tried to dissuade him. The official was firm, however, in his determination to go if the king would send him. With great hesitation the latter complied, and some days later the new governor arrived at the scene of the triple tragedy.

It is customary for newly appointed provincial governors to enter upon the duties of their office three days after their arrival at their posts. So this one had three days in which to set his affairs in order before assuming the reins of government. The *ajeons* looked upon him with wonder to think that he would thus brave almost certain death. The first and second nights passed without any trouble. It was the third night that was to be feared. As evening came on the governor told the *ajeons* to sleep as usual in the room adjoining his own. He ordered the great candles lit, two of them, as large around as a man's arm. He then seated himself on

---

* Low-level government officials who were employed in central and local government offices during the Joseon Dynasty.

his cushion, completely dressed, folded his arms, and awaited developments. The door between him and the *ajeons* was nearly shut, but a crack an inch wide gave them an opportunity to peep in from time to time and see what was going on. Not one of them closed his eyes in sleep. They feared not only for the governor but for themselves as well.

Hour after hour passed and still the governor sat as mute as a statue but wide awake. At about midnight a wave of freezing cold swept through the house. Each *ajeon* shivered like a leaf, not from cold alone but because they knew that this heralded the coming of a spirit from the dead. The candles flared wildly but did not go out, as is usually the case when spirits walk abroad.

One of the *ajeons*, braver than the rest, crept to the governor's door and looked through the crack. There sat the governor as calm as ever while in the center of the room stood the figure of a beautiful girl clad in rich garments. One hand was pressed to her bosom and the other was stretched out toward the governor as if in supplication. Her face was as white as marble, and about it played a dim mysterious light, as if from another world. The *ajeon* could not make out much of the conversation, for it was almost finished when he looked. Presently the figure of the girl faded away into a dark corner of the room, the icy pall lifted, and she was gone.

The governor called the *ajeons* in and told them

they had no need to fear longer, that the three former governors had evidently been frightened to death by this apparition but that there was no more danger. He bade them all lie down in his room and sleep. The rest of the night passed quietly.

In the morning the governor assumed the duties of his office, and his first command was to send to the town of Chilwon, arrest the head *ajeon*, tell him that all was known, and wrest a confession from him by torture.

This was done, and the wretch confessed that in order to secure his dead brother's estate, he had killed that brother's only daughter and buried her behind his house. The body, being disinterred, was found to be perfectly preserved. It was given decent burial and the wicked *ajeon* was killed.

So the spirit of the girl was laid, and no more governors were frightened to death by her appeals for justice. In later years this same governor was second-in-command of the military expedition against the traitor Yi Gwal, who had raised a dangerous insurrection in the north. This was early in the seventeenth century. It is said that the spirit of this girl used to appear to him each night and tell him how to dispose his troops upon the morrow so as to defeat the rebel. The general-in-chief acted upon his suggestions, and thus it was that this formidable rebellion was so easily put down.

HEN VERSUS CENTIPEDE

Song Gu-yun was a modest man, as well he might be, since he was only a *yeoriggun*, or runner for one of the silk shops at Jongno. His business was to stand on the street and, with persuasive tones, induce the passerby to change his mind and buy a bolt of silk rather than something else he had in mind.

One day a slave woman came along and let him lead her into the silk shop. He did not expect he would get much of a percentage out of what such a woman would buy, but it would be better than nothing. When she had looked over the goods, however, she bought lavishly and paid in good hard cash. A few days later she came again and would listen to no other *yeoriggun* but Song, who felt much flattered. Again she bought heavily, and Song began to hear the money jingle in his pouch. So it went on day after day until the other runners were green with envy. At last the slave woman said that her mistress would like to see him about some important purchases, and Song followed her to the eastern part of the city, where they entered a fine large house. Song was ushered immediately into the presence of the mistress of the house, rather to his embarrassment, for, as we have said, Song was a modest man, and this procedure was a little out of the ordinary for Korea. But the lady set him at his ease immediately by thanking him for having been of such help in making former purchases and by entering upon the details of others that she intended. Song had to spend all his time running between her house and the shops.

One day the lady inquired about his home and prospects and, learning that he was a childless widower, suggested that he occupy a part of her house so as to be more conveniently situated for the work she had for him. He gratefully accepted the offer, and things kept going from bad to worse, or rather from good to better, until at last he married the woman and settled down to a life of comparative ease.

But his felicity was rudely shocked. One night as he was going homeward from Jongno along the side of the sewer below Water Gauge Bridge, he heard his dead father's voice calling to him out of the air and saying, "Listen, my son, you must kill the woman though she is beautiful and seems good. Kill her as you would a reptile."

Song stood still in mute astonishment. It was indeed his father's voice and had told him to kill the good woman who had taken him out of his poverty and made him wealthy, who had been a kind and loving wife for more than a year. No, he could not kill her. It was absurd.

The next night he passed the same way and again he heard the weird voice calling as if from a distance, "Kill her, kill her like a reptile. Kill her before the seventeenth of the moon at dusk or you yourself will die." This gave Song a nervous chill. It was so horribly definite, the seventeenth at dusk. That was only ten days off. Well, he would think it over. But the more he thought about it, the less possible it seemed, to take the life of his innocent wife. He put the thought away, and for some days shunned the place where, alone, the voice was heard. On the night of the sixteenth he passed that way and this time the unearthly voice fairly screamed at him. "Why don't you do my bidding? I say, kill her or you will die tomorrow. Forget her goodness, look not upon her beauty. Kill her as you would a serpent; kill her—kill, kill!"

This time Song fairly made up his mind to obey the voice, and he went home sad at heart because of the horrible crime that his father was driving him to. When, however, he entered the house and his wife greeted him, hung up his hat, and brought his favorite pipe, his grim determination began to melt away, and inside of an hour he had decided that, father or no father, he could not and would not destroy this woman. He was sure he would have to die for it, but why not? She had done everything for him, and if one of them must die, why should it not be he rather than his benefactress? This generous thought stayed with him all the following day, and when the afternoon shadows began to lengthen, he made his way homeward with a stout heart. If he was to die at dusk he might as well do so decently at home. Everything was just as usual there. His wife was as kind and gentle as she always had been, and sudden death seemed the very last thing that could happen.

As the fatal moment approached, however, his wife fell silent and then got up and moved to the farther side of the room and sat down in a dark corner. Song looked steadily at her. He was so fortified in his mind because of his entire honesty of purpose that no thought of fear troubled him. He looked at her steadily, and as he looked, that beautiful, mobile face began to change. The smile that had always been there turned to a demon's scowl. The fair features turned a sickly green. The eyes glared with the same wild light that shines in a tiger's eyes. She was not looking at him but away toward another corner of the room. She bent forward, her hands clutching at the air and her head working up and down and backward and forward as though she were struggling for breath. Every fiber of her frame was tense to the point of breaking, and her whole being seemed enveloped and absorbed in some hateful and deadly atmosphere. The climax came and passed, and Song saw his wife fall forward on her face with a shudder and a groan and lie there in a state of unconsciousness. But he never moved a muscle. He felt no premonition of death and would simply wait until the queer drama was acted out to a finish.

An hour passed and then he heard a long-drawn sigh, and his wife opened her eyes. The frenzy was all gone as well as all the other evil symptoms. She sat up and passed her hand across her brow as if to wipe away the memory of a dream. Then she came to, sat down beside her husband, and took his hand.

"Why did you not do as your father's voice ordered?" Song gave a violent start. How should she know?

"What—what do you mean?" he stammered, but she only smiled gravely and said:

"You heard your father's voice telling you to kill me but you would not do it; and now let me tell you what it all really means. You have acted rightly. Your own better nature prevailed and frustrated a most diabolical plot. That was not your father's voice at all but the voice of a wizard fowl that has been seeking my destruction for three hundred years. Don't look incredulous, for I am telling you the truth. Now listen. For many a long century I was a centipede, but after passing my thousandth year I attained the power to assume the human shape. But, as you know, the hen and the centipede are deadly enemies, and there was a cock that had lived nearly as long as I but never succeeded in killing me. At last I became a woman, and then the only way to kill me was to induce some man to do it. This is why the cock assumed your father's voice and called to you and urged you to kill me. He knew that on this night at dusk he must have his last fight with me, and he knew that he must lose. So he sought to make you kill me in advance. You refused, and what you have just witnessed was my final conflict with him. I have won, and as my reward for winning I can now entirely cast off my former state and be simply a woman. Your faith and generosity have saved me. When you go to your office tomorrow morning, go at an early hour, and as you pass the place where you heard the voice, look down into the sewer and you shall see, if you need further evidence, that what I say is true."

Song assured her that he needed no further proof, and yet when morning came he showed that curiosity is not a monopoly of the fairer sex by rising early and hurrying up the street. He turned in at the Water Gauge Bridge and passed up alongside the sewer. He looked down, and there at the bottom lay an enormous white cock that had lived over four centuries but now had been vanquished. It was as large as a ten-year-old child, and had it lived a few years longer it would have attained the power to assume human shape. Song shuddered to think how near he had come to killing his sweet wife, and from that day on he never ate chickens but set his teeth into them with extraordinary zest.

A Tiger Hunter's Revenge

Sung-yangi was a small school boy in the far north of Korea in the town of Kanggye some three centuries ago, but though he was a diligent student, his school life did not run smoothly. The boys were always teasing him because he had no father. One would say in a stage whisper, "Aha, he has no father. Perhaps he never had one." Another would say, "Perhaps he has run away." Another still would drop dark hints about a possible crime.

At last it became unendurable, and the little fellow went home to his mother and announced that he was going to commit suicide. He went and found the family butcher knife and said he was going to let out his life with it. His mother sprang toward him and caught him by the wrist.

"What do you mean? Why are you trying to take your life?" The boy then told her the innuendoes that his mates had been putting out, but his mother stopped him and said:

"I will tell you all about your father. He was a mighty hunter. His fame spread all over northern Korea. At a hundred paces he could hit with his arrow any one of the prongs of a spear. His fate was a sad one, and I have never told it to you, but now you shall hear. One day he went away to hunt as usual but did not return. I waited month after month, but he never came. At last a wood gatherer came bringing a torn and bloodstained garment that I recognized as your father's. Then I knew that a tiger had eaten him. Four months after he disappeared, you were born, and I decided that I would not tell you of your father's fate till you were old enough to seek revenge for it, but now you are only nine years old and I have had to tell you." The child stood still with a scowl on his face for a minute and then turned and walked away. The school saw him no more, but he secured a bow and some arrows and every day he would go into the woods and practice from dawn till dark. This he kept up till his seventeenth year, when he had surpassed even his father in his skill at archery. He could hit a spot an inch in diameter at a hundred and twenty paces. He was already fully grown.

One morning he announced to his mother that he was going to set out to seek revenge for his father's untimely death. He sped away through the forests till he had left all habitations far behind. He was in the midst of the pathless primeval forests of the northern Pyeongan-do.

As he was forcing his way through the thick underbrush, he came upon a little hut where he found a very old man. They were both about equally surprised, but when he told his errand the old man praised him highly and said:

"I have had eight sons. Seven of them grew to be so strong that they could toss huge stones about as you would toss jujubes, but the tigers killed every one of them, and I have only my youngest son left. If you are going to fight the tigers I will give you four things to help you: namely, medicine, a treasure, a stratagem, and a helper." So saying he drew out a stout box and produced some mountain ginseng, which will sustain life for months, as everyone knows. Next he produced a *bisu*. Now a *bisu* is a knife so well tempered and so keen that all you have to do is shake it at a man and he will be cut all to pieces, without it ever touching his body. Then he brought out a black garment that would cover the whole body, excepting the eyes, and make a person invisible—all but the eyes. For the fourth gift the old man led out his only remaining son and said that he should go as the helper of the young hunter.

Sung-yangi thanked the old man profusely, and the next morning early the two young fellows started out on the quest for a double revenge—one for his father and the other for his seven brothers.

They plunged into the woods again and, after two days' tramp, approached the place that was reported to be the home of the tigers, the central citadel from which they went forth to harry the countryside. As they approached this rugged spot, they moved very cautiously, and before crossing the summit of a ridge they would crawl to the top and take a careful look over before showing themselves. As they were thus engaged, on the third day out they peeped over the summit of a rocky ledge and, to their surprise, saw a beautiful house nestled in the valley between two hills. They lay very still and watched for an hour or more, and at last they saw a Buddhist nun emerge from the building and make her way toward a spring of water at the rear. The moment they saw her, the young hunter's suspicions were aroused. What meant this beautiful house here in the midst of this forest? And besides, the old man had told him that tigers did not always go about in tiger's skins but often assumed the appearance of a Buddhist monk. So he told his companion to lie in the bushes with his hand on the bowstring and when he should hear the tinkling of the little bell, he should shoot. This bell was one that

Sung-yangi wore at his belt for this very purpose. Then the young fellow stalked boldly out and accosted the old woman. She was somewhat terrified at his sudden appearance, but as soon as she regained her composure she begged him to give her some tinder with which to light a fire, as her's was all gone. He gave her a little and she hurried home with it but soon returned, saying she had used it but the fire would not burn; she begged for a little more. The boy gave it but again she came and asked for more. This was what he had been waiting for. He knew that if he lost his tinder and could not start a fire, he would starve in the woods, and he saw that the old nun was trying to get all his away.

Suddenly his hand went to his belt, the little bell tinkled, and an arrow came whizzing from the bushes and struck the nun in the side. Instantly her form changed to that of an enormous tiger, and with a roar that made the very mountains tremble, she rose on her hind feet and made a spring at Sung-yangi. But he was ready for her, and while she was in mid-air an arrow from his bow sped true to its mark and pierced her heart.

This done, Sung-yangi donned the black suit that made him invisible and entered the gateway of the beautiful house. There he found five old monks looking about in a dazed way and wondering what was the cause of the terrific roar they had first heard, and to add to their dismay they saw a pair of eyes, as if they were in mid-air, glaring at them. This pair of glittering eyes circled round them about six feet from the ground and gave them what is commonly known as "the creeps."

But they did not remain long in doubt, for soon arrows began to fly from some invisible source, and as each of them found its mark, a monk leaped in the air and fell to earth—a beautiful striped tiger. Sung-yangi thereupon doffed his magic garments and called in his companion, and together they searched the buildings thoroughly to discover whether their revenge was complete or whether some of their enemies were in hiding. As they were passing through the kitchen they met a young woman who appeared to be a domestic servant, but they were most astonished to find her in such a place, for even if the dwellers in the house had been respectable people it would have been no place for her. However, she offered no explanation but simply invited them to be seated in the reception room until she could finish preparing them some food. This seemed a reasonable proposition, and in a little while she came in with two bowls of some kind of soup. The smell was very appetizing, but when Sung-yangi looked in his bowl he saw a piece of skin with what looked like a piece of human hair attached. He turned to the young woman and demanded what it meant. She bowed low and in a faltering voice confessed that they had nothing in the place but human flesh for food. She then pointed to the rafters, where hung thousands of little wooden tags with names written on them. "There," she said "you see the *hopae* (Every male citizen is obliged by law to carry on his person a wooden name tag with his name and place of residence for purposes of identification) of all the people that the tigers living here have slain and eaten. They always preserve the tags as memoranda of the events and for purposes of reference."

Sang-yangi looked upon the horrid mementoes and shuddered but forced himself to examine them carefully, and before long he came upon one that made him utter an exclamation of grief and horror. It was the name tag of his own father. So he knew that he had come to the right place to secure his revenge. When his companion saw this, he also searched through the tags and found the names of all his murdered brothers.

That night both of the young men had dreams. Sung-yangi was visited by the shade of his father, who praised him for his perseverance and bravery and placed in his hands a map and a sealed letter, telling him that the former was a map that would show him the best and shortest way out of the forest and that the second was not to be opened till he arrived at his home. The other dream showed the boy his seven brothers, who came and gave him a letter to be opened only in his father's presence. Sung-yangi's father also told him that the young woman had been sent by himself to enable them to find the name tags and thus the evidence that their revenge was complete.

In the morning the proof of the genuineness of the dreams lay there on the floor in the shape of two letters and a map. The young woman was nowhere to be found. With his wonderful knife, Sung-yangi flayed the dead tigers in a trice, and together the two boys made their way out of the forest. Both the letters advised the young men to give up hunting as an occupation.

How Jin Outwitted
the Devils

In the good old days, before the skirts of Joseon were
defiled by contact with the outer world and before the
bird-twittering voice of the foreigner was heard in the
land, the "curfew tolled the knell of parting day," to
some effect. There was a special set of police called *sulla*
whose business it was to see that no stray samples of
male humanity were on the streets after the great bell
had ceased its grumbling. Each of these watchmen was
on duty every other night, but if on any night any one
of them failed to "run in" a belated pedestrian, it was
counted to him for lack of constabulary zeal and he
would be compelled to go on his beat the next night and
every successive night until he did succeed in capturing

a victim. Talk about police regulations! Here was a rule that for pure knowledge of human nature put to shame anything that Solon and Draco could have concocted between them. Tell every policeman on the Bowery that he can't come off his beat till he has arrested some genuine offender and the Augean stables would be nothing to what they would accomplish in a week's time.

Such was the strenuous mission of Jin Ga-dong. One night it was his fate to suffer for his last night's failure to spot a victim. He prowled about like a cat till the wee hours, and then, having failed to catch his mouse, ascended the upper story of the East Gate to find a place where he could take a nap. He looked over the parapet and there he saw, seated on the top of the outer wall which forms a sort of curtain for the gate, three hideous forms in the moonlight. They were not human, surely, but Jin, like all good policemen, was *sans peur* even if he was not *sans reproche*, and so he hailed the gruesome trio and demanded their business.

"We're straight from hell," said they, "and we are ordered to summon before his infernal majesty the soul of Plum Blossom, only daughter of Big Man Kim of Schoolhouse Ward, Pagoda Place, third street to the right, second blind alley on the left, two doors beyond the wineshop."

Then they hurried away on their mission, leaving Jin to digest their strange news. He was possessed of a strong desire to follow them and see what would happen. Sleep was out of the question, and he might run across a stray pedestrian, so he hurried up the street to Schoolhouse Ward, turning down Pagoda Place and then up the third street to the right and into the second blind alley to the left, and there he saw the basket on a bamboo pole which betokened the wineshop. Two doors beyond, he stopped and listened at the gate. Something was going on within, of a surety, for the sound of anxious voices and hurrying feet were heard, and presently a man came out and put down the alley at a lively pace. Jin followed swiftly and soon had his hand on the man's collar.

"I'm afraid you're caught this time, my man. This is a late hour to be out."

"Oh, please let me go. I am after a doctor. The only daughter of my master is suddenly ill and everything depends on my haste."

"Come back," said Jin in an authoritative voice. "I know all about the case. The girl's name is Plum Blossom, and your master's name is Big Man Kim. The spirits have come to take her, but I can thwart them if you come back quickly and get me into the house."

The man was speechless with amazement and fear at Jin's uncanny knowledge of the whole affair, and he dared not disobey. Back they came, and the servant smuggled the policeman in by a side door. It was a desperate case. The girl was *in extremis* and the parents consented to let Jin in as a last chance.

On entering the room where the girl lay, he saw the three fiends ranged against the opposite wall, though none of the others could see them. They winked at him in an exasperatingly familiar way and fingered the earthenware bottles in their hands, intimating that they were waiting to take the girl's soul to the nether regions in these receptacles. The moment had arrived, and they simultaneously drew the stoppers from their bottles and held them toward the inanimate form on the bed.

But Jin was a man of action. His billy was out in an instant, and with it he struck a sweeping blow that smashed the three bottles to flinders and sent them crashing into the corner. The fiends fled through a crack in the window with a howl and left Jin alone with the dead—no, not dead, for the girl turned her head and, with a sigh, fell into a healthful slumber.

It is hardly necessary to say that Jin was speedily promoted from *sulla* to the position of son-in-law to Big Man Kim.

But he had not heard the last of the devil's trio. They naturally thirsted for revenge and bit their fingernails to the quick devising some especially exquisite torment for him when they should have him in their clutches. The time came when they could wait no longer, and though the *Book of Human Life* showed that his time had not come, they secured permission to secure him if possible.

At the dead of night he awoke and saw their eyes gleaming at him through the darkness. He was unprepared for resistance and had to go with them. The way led through a desert country over a stony road. Jin kept his wits at work and finally opened a conversation with his captors.

"I suppose that you fiends never feel fear." "No," they answered, "nothing can frighten us." But they looked at each other as much as to say, "We might tell something if we would."

"But surely there must be something that you hold in dread. Yon are not supreme, and if there is nothing that you fear it argues that you are lacking in intelligence."

Piqued at this dispraise, one of them said, "If I tell you, what difference will it make, anyway? We have you now securely. There are, in truth, only two things that we fear, namely the wood of the *eum* tree and the hairlike grass called *gimipul*. Now tell us what you in turn most dread."

"Well," answered Jin, "it may seem strange, but my greatest aversion is a big bowl of white rice with sauerkraut* and boiled pig on the side and a beaker of white beer** at my elbow. These invariably conquer me." The fiends made a mental note.

––––––––––

* A reference to kimchi.
** I.e., *makgeolli*.

And so they fared along toward the regions of the dead until they came to a field in which an *eum* tree was growing. The fiends crouched and hurried by, but Jin, by a single bound, placed himself beneath its shade and there, to his delight, found some of the hairlike grass growing. He snatched it up by handfuls and decorated his person with it before the fiends had recovered from their first astonishment.

They dared not approach and seize him, for he was protected by the tree and the grass, but after a hurried consultation, two of them sped away on some errand while the other stayed to watch their prey. An hour later, back came the two, bearing a table loaded with the very things that Jin had named as being fatal to him. There was the white rice, the redolent sauerkraut, the succulent pig, and the flagon of milk-white beer. The fiends came and placed these things as near as they dared and then retired to a safe distance to watch his undoing. Jin fell to and showed the power that these toothsome things had over him, and when the fiends came to seize him, he broke a limb off the tree and belabored them so that they fled screaming and disappeared over the horizon. So Jin's spirit went back to his body, and he lived again. He had long been aware of some such danger and had warned his wife that if he should die or appear to die, they should not touch his body for six days. So all was well.

Many years passed, during which Jin attained all the honors in the gift of his sovereign, and at last the time came for him to die in earnest. The same three imps came again, but very humbly. He laughed and said he was ready now to go. Again they traveled the long road, but Jin was aware that they would try to steer him into hell rather than let him attain to heaven, and he kept his eyes open.

One afternoon Jin forged ahead of his three conductors and came to a place where the road branched in three directions. One of the roads was rough, one smooth, and on the other a woman sat beside a brook pounding clothes. He hailed her and asked which was the road to heaven. She said the smooth one, and before his guards came up, Jin was out of sight on the road to Elysium. He knew they would be after him, hot foot, so when he saw twelve men sitting beside the road with masks on their faces, he joined them and asked if they did not have an extra mask. They produced one, and Jin, instead of taking his place at the end of the line, squeezed in about the middle and donned his mask. Presently, along came the fiends in a great hurry. They suspected the trick that Jin had played, but they saw it only in part, for they seized the end man and dragged him away to hell, where they found they had the wrong man, and the judge had to apologize profusely for the gaucherie of the fiends.

Meanwhile, the maskers were trying to decide what should be done with Jin. He was in the way and creating trouble. They finally decided that as the great stone Buddha at Ungjin in Korea was without a soul, it would be a good thing to send Jin's spirit to inhabit that image. It was done, and Jin had rest.

Jin taught the Koreans one great lesson, at least, and that was that the devils are afraid of *eum* wood and the *gimi* grass, and since his time no sensible person will fail to have a stick of that wood and a bunch of that grass hung up over his door as a notice to the imps that he is not at home.

THE GHOST OF A GHOST

A Korean country gentleman, Kim for convenience, had become a widower with a small son on his hands, and as this threw his domestic arrangements into confusion, he looked about for a number two to share his joys and sorrows and, incidentally, to cook his *bap*. In this quest he was successful, and in time another son was born. But by this time the firstborn had grown into a young man and had developed a violent dislike to his stepmother and his little half brother, and a person even less astute than the father could not fail to foresee that upon his demise the elder son would show small favor to the wife and the child.

For this reason the old gentleman, upon his deathbed,

gave to his wife a piece of paper on which was drawn a picture of a man and his son and told her to keep it with great care, and that when the time came that she could no longer make ends meet, she should take the picture to the local magistrate and ask redress. He unhesitatingly affirmed that justice would thus be done her.

Not long after this he breathed his last, and it was but a month or two later that the elder son began to show his teeth. The property was all taken from the widow, and no provision whatever was made for her support. She had only one small box in which she preserved the picture. The little boy pleaded with his big brother to help his mother but was driven from the door with blows. Finally, the unhappy woman reached the point of destitution that her husband had foreseen, and, taking the picture, she went to the office of the prefect and told her story.

The prefect looked long and intently at the piece of paper, studied it from every point of view, but said at last that he could make nothing out of it. The enigma was too deep for him. He told her to leave the picture with him overnight, and he would think it over. As he pondered the matter he concluded there must be some solution and was piqued at his own inability to find it. Late into the night he sat and thought about it, but the more he thought the more insoluble became the riddle. About midnight he called his servant and ordered a bowl of water. After drinking a little, he set the bowl down, but in doing so a portion of the water was spilled upon the picture that lay on the floor beside him. He was startled, for this might injure the picture and render the solution wholly impossible, so he picked up the paper carefully and held it near the candle flame to dry it, when lo! the riddle solved itself. The porous paper was made semitransparent by the water, and the light, shining through, revealed a written communication concealed between the two thicknesses of paper which formed the substance of the picture. He glanced around to see whether his servant had noticed it and was relieved to find that he alone was the possessor of the secret. His first act was to destroy the picture, after which he retired as usual.

In the morning when the *ajeons* came to pay their respects, he ordered one of them to go down to the house of the man who had treated his stepmother so badly and announce that the prefect would call there at two in the afternoon. This created something of a sensation, and when the prefect arrived, he found the place swept and garnished. Quite a crowd of the townspeople had gathered out of curiosity to see what this visit might portend.

As the prefect entered the gate, he saw the master of the house and the others gathered about the steps of the *sarang* (reception room), but on the left the yard was empty. The host came forward to greet him, but, strange to say, the prefect waved him aside and looked intently to the left. Then, folding the front part of his coat about him as the Korean does in the presence of a superior, he advanced a few steps toward the left, bent forward in a deferential manner and said:

"Yes, certainly no, never before without doubt . . . Oh no, no I could not think of it . . . yes, quite sure . . . no difficulty whatever . . . It shall be done at once . . . Indeed I shall not forget."

All this in reply to apparently unheard questions of an unseen interlocutor! The people stood openmouthed with wonder. Had the prefect indeed gone mad? But the play was not yet finished. The prefect went toward the gate as if taking leave of someone, said good-bye with the utmost deference, and then came back to the amazed group of spectators and said:

"Who was that man?" They hesitated, but at last one of them made bold to answer:

"There was no one there."

"What—? That man I was just talking to and who has just gone? You didn't see him?"

"No, we saw no one nor did we hear anything but your words."

"Amazing! Wonderful! Astounding! I saw an elderly gentleman standing there, and he had the air of a great official. He spoke to me and said that in this town his widow and her little boy were suffering because the grown-up son had defrauded them of their rights. He told me he had foreseen this and had buried beneath the floor of that deserted house, over there, three caskets of silver and two of gold for the use of his widow. He told me to take two of the silver caskets and give the rest to his widow. And you never saw him! Well, well, it was a singular hallucination. Let us think no more about it."

But what company of people would rest satisfied with this? They protested that there must be some reason behind the vision and urged the prefect to dig for the treasure. He demurred and said it was foolish but was finally persuaded. Mattocks were secured and they all hastened to the deserted house where, sure enough, the caskets were unearthed. Instead of thinking the prefect was crazy they now concluded that he was inspired. He took it very modestly and, calling the widow and her son, turned over the valuable treasure to them.

"The old gentleman told me to keep two of the silver caskets for myself, but I am going to venture to disobey him and keep only one."

A murmur of admiration went around the company, and they and the woman begged him to take two, but he protested that even the fear of the spirits' anger would not induce him to take more than one.

Thus the woman was vindicated, the prefect enveloped in the odor of sanctity, and his exchequer replenished, for the writing in the picture had only revealed the position of the buried treasure but had made no provision for the prefect's squeeze.

THE TENTH SCION[*]

Long, long ago there existed a family of learned men;
there had been nine generations and in every one of
them one only son. Each man had no sooner passed his
examinations and taken his degree than he died. Thus
the tenth generation had been reached, which again
consisted only of one single representative.

Now, when this tenth scion was ten years old, there
came one day a monk to the house to beg alms. The
mother sent her son to hand the alms to the monk. The
latter looked the boy for a moment in the face and said:

---

[*] Translated by Rev. G. Engel.

"Poor boy, thou art in a bad case."

When the boy heard this, he ran to his mother and told her what the monk had said, and she at once sent a servant after the monk to recall him.

Being asked the reason of his strange exclamation, the monk replied: "When the little monk looks into the boy's face, it seems to him that the child will be killed at the age of fifteen by a wild beast. Should he, however, escape the disaster, he will become a great man."

The lady then inquired how the evil could be warded off. The monk replied: "It will be best to get the boy's traveling kit ready at once and to let him go wherever he likes."

Whereupon the widows (mother, grandmother, and great-grandmother), after embracing the boy and weeping bitterly, sent him away according to the monk's word.

As the boy did not know where to go, he simply wandered in this and that direction. Thus the time passed quickly, and in a twinkle his fifteenth year had arrived.

One day he strayed from the main road and lost his bearings. He inquired of a passerby: "Will I be able to reach human dwellings if I go in this direction?"

The man replied, "There are no human dwellings in these hills except a monastery. But a great calamity has befallen it, all the monks have died, and it stands empty now. Whoever enters its precincts is doomed to death."

Innumerable times did the man try to dissuade him from going. But try as he would, the boy, having conceived the wish to go there by hook or by crook, set out for the monastery.

When he reached it, he found it exactly as the man had told him: it was empty throughout. As it was winter just then and the weather very cold, he searched for charcoal and, when he had found some, made a blazing fire in a firebox. He then mounted with it to the garret above the Buddha image in the central hall and thus made himself invisible to any unforeseen caller.

After the third watch (after 1 a.m.), there arose a great uproar. He peeped stealthily down and saw a crowd of animals enter. There were a tiger, a rabbit, a fox, and a great many other animals. Each one took its place, and when they were all seated, the tiger addressed the rabbit: "Doctor Rabbit!" (The rabbit is thought by Koreans to be the learned one among the animals.) Receiving a ready response, he continued: "Will the professor turn up a page of prophecy tonight and let us know whether we shall have success or failure?"

The rabbit assented, pulled a small book from under the mat on which he was sitting, read in it, and, after meditating a long while, announced his discovery: "Tonight the diagrams are strange."

"How is that?" asked the tiger.

"The prophecy runs as follows," replied the rabbit.

"Sir Tiger will receive heaven-fire (heaven-fire is also equivalent to "great disaster") and Master Rabbit will meet with the loss of his goods."

Scarcely had he said the words when the boy threw a few live coals down on the tiger. This created such terror among the animals that they all took to flight.

The boy descended from the loft and, on looking about, found the little book out of which the rabbit had been reading. He picked it up and wondered whether he would, after such a find, meet with his predicted misfortune.

He at once went outside the gate of the monastery, looked about in all directions, and noticed a light gleaming in a mountain valley towards the east. Thinking there was a human dwelling there, he set out in that direction and found a one-room straw hut.

When he called out for the master of the house, there appeared a maiden of sweet sixteen who welcomed him without any embarrassment. Thinking this a lucky circumstance, he entered the hut.

He began to tell the girl about his past life. But as he was very tired, he lay down while the girl sat and did some needlework. Now, when she was threading her needle, she moistened her finger with her tongue, and he noticed, to his horror, that it was a black thread-like tongue, like a snake's.

This discovery set him all atremble, and he was

thinking of running away, when the "thing," guessing his intention, said, "Although you escaped the former calamities, you shall not escape me yet. Before the bell in the monastery behind here rings three times you shall have become my food."

Now, while the boy was inwardly sorrowing and expecting his death every minute, the bell rang all of a sudden three times. The girl had no sooner heard it than she threw herself at his feet and implored him for her life.

He, pretending to possess immense power, shouted at her in the most imposing manner he could muster. The "thing" then drew a square gem from its side, offered it to him, and again pleaded with him for her life.

He took the gem and asked what it was. She replied, "If you strike one corner and say, 'Money, come out!' money will appear. If you strike the second and say to a dead person, 'Live!' he will rise at once. By striking the third you can produce whatever you wish."

As she stopped and did not give any explanation about the fourth comer, he asked her, "What does this corner do?"

When it seemed as though she was never going to tell him, he said to her: "Only if you tell me about this fourth comer will I let you go."

Then, as he insisted on getting an answer, she could no longer refuse and replied, "If you say to hateful people, 'Die!' they die."

At once the boy pointed at her and cried, "Above all you are the most hateful to me. DIE!" Scarcely had he uttered the words when a huge snake as thick as a pillar rolled at his feet and died. This gave him such a fright that he left the house at once.

As he was anxious to find out what could have made the bell ring so suddenly, he went back to the monastery and found a cock pheasant with a stone in its beak lying dead in front of the bell.

But what had this pheasant to do with him? As he tried to recollect the past, he remembered that when he was seven or eight years old, he had one day gone with a servant up the hill near his house and found a cock pheasant that, being pursued by a hawk, had hid itself in the pine thicket. The servant had been for killing and eating the bird. But as he had cried with all his might and begged for it, the servant had, after warning him several times not to let it go, given it to him. He had taken it in his arms and admired it. The sheen of its feathers had been just dazzling, and he had thought it was altogether very beautiful to look at and would make a splendid toy. But then the pheasant had looked as though it had been shedding tears, and out of pity he had let it fly.

"Now," he said to himself, "without doubt, the pheasant has remembered that kindness, and when I was near dying, it saved me." Weeping bitterly, the boy took off his waistcoat, wrapped the bird in it, and buried it in a sunny spot.

In this way he had passed his fifteenth year and become sixteen years old, and it seemed to him that his fatal period was now ended. He therefore went to his native place and showed himself before his mother.

You should have seen the fuss they made about him. His mother, grandmother, and great-grandmother laughed and cried in turn. Their sobs shook them so that one would have thought it was a house of mourning.

By and by the boy was married, had three sons, and became, so they say, the founder of a great family.

PART II

THE STORY OF JANG DORYEONG

In the days of King Jungjong (r. 1506–1544) there lived a beggar in Seoul whose face was extremely ugly and always dirty. He was forty years of age or so but still wore his hair down his back like an unmarried boy. He carried a bag over his shoulder and went about the streets begging. During the day he went from one part of the city to the other, visiting each section, and when night came on he would huddle up beside someone's gate and go to sleep. He was frequently seen in Jongno (Bell Street) in company with the servants and underlings of the rich. They were great friends, he and they, joking and bantering as they met. He used to say that his name was Jang, and so they called him Jang Doryeong, *doryeong* meaning an unmarried boy, son of the gentry. At that time the magician Jeon U-chi—who was far-famed for his pride and arrogance—whenever he met Jang in passing along the street, would dismount and prostrate himself most humbly. Not only did he bow, but he seemed to regard Jang with the greatest of fear, so that he dared not look him in the face. Jang, sometimes, without even inclining his head, would say, "Well, how goes it with you, eh?" Jeon, with his hands in his sleeves, would reply most respectfully, "Very well, sir, thank you, very well." He had fear written on all his features when he faced Jang. Sometimes, too, when Jeon would bow, Jang would refuse to notice him at all and go by without a word. Those who saw it were astonished, and asked Jeon the reason. Jeon said in reply, "There are only three spirit men at present in Joseon, of whom the greatest is Jang Doryeong; the second is Jeong Buk-chang; and the third is Yun Se-pyeong. People of the world do not know it, but I do. Such being the case, should I not bow before him and show him reverence?"

Those who heard this explanation, knowing that Jeon himself was a strange being, paid no attention to it. At that time in Seoul there was a certain literary undergraduate in office whose house joined hard on the street. This man used to see Jang frequently going about begging, and one day he called him and asked who he was and why he begged. Jang made answer,

"I was originally of a cultured family of Jeolla-do, but my parents died of typhus fever, and I had no brothers or relations left to share my lot. I alone remained of all my clan, and having no home of my own I have gone about begging, and have at last reached Seoul. As I am not skilled in any handicraft and do not know Chinese letters, what else can I do?" The undergraduate, hearing that he was from a cultured family, felt very sorry for him, gave him food and drink, and refreshed him.

From this time on, whenever there was any special celebration at his home, he used to call Jang in and have him share it. On a certain day when the master was on his way to the office, he saw a dead body being carried on a stretcher off toward the Water Gate. Looking at it closely from the horse on which he rode, he recognized it as the corpse of Jang Doryeong. He felt so sad that he turned back to his house and cried over it, saying, "There are lots of miserable people on earth, but who ever saw one as miserable as poor Jang? As I reckon the time over on my fingers, he has been begging in Bell Street for fifteen years, and now he passes out of the city a dead body."

Twenty years and more afterwards the master had to make a journey through Jeollanam-do. As he was passing Mt. Jirisan, he lost his way and got into a maze among the hills. The day began to wane, and he could neither return nor go forward. He saw a narrow footpath, such as woodsmen take, and turned into it to see if it led to any habitation. As he went along there were rocks and deep ravines. Little by little, as he advanced farther, the scene changed and seemed to become strangely transfigured. The farther he went the more wonderful it became. After he had gone some miles, he discovered himself to be in another world entirely, no longer a world of earth and dust. He saw someone coming toward him dressed in ethereal green, mounted and carrying a shade, with servants accompanying. He seemed to sweep toward him with swiftness and without effort. He thought to himself, "Here is some high lord or other coming to meet me, but," he added, "how among these deeps and solitudes could a gentleman come riding so?" He led his horse aside and tried to withdraw into one of the groves by the side of the way, but before he could think to turn the man had reached him. The mysterious stranger lifted his two hands in salutation and inquired respectfully as to how he had been all this time. The master was speechless, and so astonished that he could make no reply. But the stranger smilingly said, "My house is quite near here; come with me and rest."

He turned and, leading the way, seemed to glide and not to walk, while the master followed. At last they reached the place indicated. He suddenly saw before him great palace halls filling whole squares of space. Beautiful buildings they were, richly ornamented.

Attendants in official robes awaited them before the door. They bowed to the master and led him into the hall. After passing a number of gorgeous, palace-like rooms, he arrived at a special one and ascended to the upper story, where he met a very wonderful person. He was dressed in shining garments, and the servants that waited on him were exceedingly fair. There were, too, children about, so exquisitely beautiful that it seemed none other than a celestial palace. The master, alarmed at finding himself in such a place, hurried forward and made a low obeisance, not daring to lift his eyes. But the host smiled upon him, raised his hands, and asked, "Do you not know me? Look now." Lifting his eyes, he then saw that it was the same person who had come riding out to meet him, but he could not tell who he was. "I see you," said he, "but as to who you are I cannot tell." The kingly host then said, "I am Jang Doryeong. Do you not know me?" Then, as the master looked more closely at him, he could see the same features. The outlines of the face were there, but all the imperfections had gone, and only beauty remained. So wonderful was it that he was quite overcome.

A great feast was prepared, and the honored guest was entertained. Such food, too, was placed before him as was never seen on earth. Angelic beings played on beautiful instruments and danced as no mortal eye ever looked upon. Their faces, too, were like pearls and precious stones.

Jang Doryeong said to his guest, "There are four famous mountains in Korea in which the genii reside. This hill is one. In days gone by, for a fault of mine, I was exiled to earth, and in the time of my exile you treated me with marked kindness, a favor that I have never forgotten. When you saw my dead body your pity went out to me; this, too, I remember. I was not dead then, it was simply that my days of exile were ended and I was returning home. I knew that you were passing this hill, and I desired to meet you and thank you for all your kindness. Your treatment of me in another world is sufficient to bring about our meeting in this one." And so they met and feasted in joy and great delight.

When night came he was escorted to a special pavilion, where he was to sleep. The windows were made of jade and precious stones, and soft lights came streaming through them so that there was no night. "My body was so rested and my soul so refreshed," said he, "that I felt no need of sleep."

When the day dawned a new feast was spread, and then farewells were spoken. Jang said, "This is not a place for you to stay long in; you must go. The ways differ of we genii and you men of the world. It will be difficult for us ever to meet again. Take good care of yourself and go in peace." He then called a servant to accompany him and show the way. The master made a low bow and withdrew. When he had gone but a short distance, he suddenly found himself in the old world with its dusty accompaniments. The path by which he came out was not the way by which he had entered. In order to mark the entrance he planted a stake, and then the servant withdrew and disappeared.

The year following the master went again and tried to find the citadel of the genii, but there were only mountain peaks and impassable ravines, and where it was he never could discover.

As the years went by the master seemed to grow younger in spirit, and at last at the age of ninety he passed away without suffering. "When Jang was here on earth and I saw him for fifteen years," said the master, "I remember but one peculiarity about him, namely, that his face never grew older nor did his dirty clothing ever wear out. He never changed his garb, and yet it never varied in appearance in all the fifteen years. This alone would have marked him as a strange being, but our fleshly eyes did not recognize it."

YUN SE-PYEONG, THE WIZARD

Yun Se-Pyeong was a military man who rose to the rank of minister in the days of King Jungjong. It seems that Yun learned the doctrine of magic from a passing stranger whom he met on his way to Peking in company with the envoy. When at home he lived in a separate house, quite apart from the other members of his family. He was a man so greatly feared that even his wife and children dared not approach him. What he did in secret no one seemed to know. In winter he was seen to put iron cleats under each arm and change them frequently, and when they were put off they seemed to be red-hot.

At the same time there was a magician in Korea called Jeon U-chi who used to go about Seoul plying his craft. So skillful was he that he could even simulate the form of the master of a house and go freely into the women's quarters. On this account he was greatly feared and detested. Yun heard of him on more than one occasion and was determined to rid the earth of him. Jeon heard also of Yun and gave him a wide berth, never appearing in his presence. He used frequently to say, "I am a magician only; Yun is a God."

On a certain day Jeon informed his wife that Yun would come that afternoon and try to kill him, "and so," said he, "I shall change my shape in order to escape his clutches. If any one comes asking for me, just say that I am not at home." He then metamorphosed himself into a beetle and crawled under a crock that stood overturned in the courtyard.

When evening began to fall, a young woman came to Jeon's house, a very beautiful woman, too, and asked, "Is the master Jeon at home?"

The wife replied, "He has just gone out."

The woman laughingly said, "Master Jeon and I have been special friends for a long time, and I have an appointment with him today. Please say to him that I have come."

Jeon's wife, seeing a pretty woman come thus and ask for her husband in such a familiar way, flew into a rage and said, "The rascal has evidently a second wife that he has never told me of. What he said just now is all false," so she went out in a fury and smashed the crock with a club. When the crock was broken, there was the beetle underneath it. Then, the woman who had called suddenly changed into a bee and flew at and stung the beetle. Jeon, metamorphosed into his accustomed form, fell over and died, and the bee flew away.

THE LITERARY MAN OF IMSIL

In the year 1654 there was a man of letters living in Imsil who claimed that he could control spirits and that two demon guards were constantly at his bidding. One day he was sitting with a friend playing chess when they agreed that the loser in each case was to pay a fine in drink. The friend lost and yet refused to pay his wager, so that the master said, "If you do not pay up I'll make it hot for you." The man, however, refused, till at last the master, exasperated, turned his back upon him and called out suddenly into the upper air some formula or other, as if he were giving a command. The man dashed off through the courtyard to make his escape, but an unseen hand bared his body and administered to him such a set of sounding blows that they left blue, seamy marks. Unable to bear the pain of it longer, he yielded, and then the master laughed and let him go.

At another time he was seated with a friend while in the adjoining village a shaman *gut* (exorcising ceremony) was in progress, with drums and gongs banging furiously. The master suddenly rushed out to the bamboo grove that stood behind the official yamen, and, looking very angry and with glaring eyes, he shouted and made bare his arm as if to drive off the furies. After a time, he ceased. The friend, thinking this a peculiar performance, asked what it meant. His reply was, "A crowd of devils has come from the *gut* and is congregating in the grove of bamboos; if I do not drive them off, trouble will follow in the town, and for that cause I shouted."

Again he was making a journey with a certain friend when, suddenly, on the way, he called out to the mid-air, saying, "Let her go, let her go, I say, or I'll have you punished severely."

His appearance was so peculiar and threatening that the friend asked the cause. For the time being he gave no answer, and they simply went on their way.

That night they entered a village where they wished to sleep, but the owner of the house said that they had sickness and asked them to go. They insisted, however, till he at last sent a servant to drive them off. Meanwhile the womenfolk watched the affair through the chinks of the window, and they talked in startled whispers, so that the scholar overheard them.

A few minutes later the man of the house followed in the most humble and abject manner, asking them to return and accept entertainment and lodging at his house. Said he, "I have a daughter, sir, and she fell ill this very day and died, and after some time came to life again. Said she, 'A devil caught me and carried my soul off down the main roadway, where we met a man, who stopped us and in fierce tones drove off the spirit, who let me go, and so I returned to life.' She looked out on your Excellency through the chink of the window, and, behold, you are the man. I am at my wits' end to know what to say to you. Are you a genii or are you a Buddhist, so marvelously to bring back the dead to life? I offer this small refreshment; please accept."

The scholar laughed and said, "Nonsense! Just a woman's haverings. How could I do such things?" He lived for seven or eight years more and died.

THE MAN ON THE ROAD

In the Manchu War of 1636, the people of Seoul rushed off in crowds to make their escape. One party of them came suddenly upon a great force of the enemy, armed and mounted. The hills and valleys seemed full of them, and there was no possible way of escape. What to do they knew not. In the midst of their perplexity they suddenly saw someone sitting peacefully in the main roadway just in front, underneath a pine tree, quite unconcerned. He had dismounted from his horse, which a servant held, standing close by. A screen of several yards of cotton cloth was hanging up just before him, as if to shield him from the dust of the passing army.

The people who were making their escape came up to

this stranger and said imploringly, "We are all doomed to die. What shall we do?"

The mysterious stranger said, "Why should you die? And why are you so frightened? Sit down by me and see the barbarians go by."

The people, perceiving his mind so composed and his appearance devoid of fear, and they having no way of escape, did as he bade them and sat down.

The cavalry of the enemy moved by in great numbers, killing everyone they met, not a single person escaping; but when they reached the place where the magician sat, they went by without, apparently, seeing anything. Thus they continued till the evening, when all had passed by. The stranger and the people with him sat the day through without any harm overtaking them, even though they were in the midst of the enemy's camp, as it were.

At last awaking to the fact that he was possessor of some wonderful magic, they all with one accord came and bowed before him, asking his name and his place of residence. He made no answer, however, but mounted his beautiful horse and rode swiftly away, no one being able to overtake him.

The day following the party fell in with a man who had been captured but had made his escape. They asked if he had seen anything special the day before. He said, "When I followed the barbarian army, passing such and such a point," indicating the place where the magician had sat with the people, "we skirted great walls and precipitous rocks, against which no one could move, and so we passed by."

Thus were the few yards of cotton cloth metamorphosed before the eyes of the passersby.

THE MAN WHO BECAME A PIG

A certain Minister of State called Kim Yu, living in the County of Seungpyeong, had a relative who resided in a far-distant part of the country, an old man aged nearly one hundred. On a certain day a son of this patriarch came to the office of the Minister and asked to see him. Kim ordered him to be admitted and inquired as to why he had come. Said he, "I have something very important to say, a private matter to lay before your Excellency. There are so many guests with you now that I'll come again in the evening and tell it."

In the evening, when all had departed, he came, and the Minister ordered out his personal retainers and asked the meaning of the call. The man replied, saying,

"My father, though very old, was, as you perhaps know, a strong and hearty man. On a certain day he called us children to him and said, 'I wish to have a siesta, so now close the door and all of you go out of the room. Do not let anyone venture in till I call you.'

"We children agreed, of course, and did so. Till late at night there was neither call nor command to open the door, so that we began to be anxious. We at last looked through the chink, and lo, there was our father changed into a huge pig! Terrified by the sight of it, we opened the door and looked in, when the animal grunted and growled and made a rush to get out past us. We hurriedly closed the door again and held a consultation.

"Some said, 'Let's keep the pig just as it is, within doors, and care for it.' Some said, 'Let's have a funeral and bury it.' We are ignorant countryfolk, not knowing just what to do under such peculiar circumstances, and so I have come to ask counsel of your Excellency. Please think over this startling phenomenon and tell us what we ought to do."

Prince Kim, hearing this, gave a great start, thought it over for a long time, and at last said, "No such mysterious thing was ever heard of before, and I really don't know what is best to do under the circumstances, but still, it seems to me that since this metamorphosis has come about, you had better not bury it before death, so give up the funeral idea. Since, too, it is not a human being any longer, I do not think it right to keep it in the house. You say that it wants to make its escape, and, as a cave in the woods or hills is its proper abode, I think you had better take it out and let it go free into the trackless depths of some mountainous country, where no foot of man has ever trod."

The son accepted this wise counsel and did as the Minister advised, taking it away into the deep mountains and letting it go. Then he donned sackcloth, mourned, buried his father's clothes for a funeral, and observed the day of metamorphosis as the day of sacrificial ceremony.

THE GRATEFUL GHOST

It is often told that in the days of the Goryeo Dynasty (918–1392), when an examination was to be held, a certain scholar came from a far-distant part of the country to take part. Once on his journey, the day was drawing to a close, and he found himself among the mountains. Suddenly, he heard a sneezing from among the creepers and bushes by the roadside but could see no one. Thinking it strange, he dismounted from his horse, went into the brake, and listened. He heard it again, and it seemed to come from the roots of the creeper close beside him, so he ordered his servant to dig round it and see. He dug and found a dead man's skull. It was full of earth, and the roots of the creeper had passed through the nostrils. The sneezing was caused by the annoyance felt by the spirit from having the nose so discommoded.

The candidate felt sorry, washed the skull in clean water, wrapped it in paper, and reburied it in its former place on the hillside. He also brought a table of food, offered sacrifice, and said a prayer.

That night, in a dream, a scholar came to him, an old man with white hair, who bowed, thanked him, and said, "On account of sin committed in a former life, I died out of season, before I had fulfilled my days. My posterity, too, were all destroyed, and my body crumbled back into the dust, my skull alone remaining, and that is what you found below the creeper. On account of the root passing through it the annoyance was great, and I could not help but sneeze. By good luck you and your kind heart, blessed of Heaven, took pity on me, buried me in a clean place, and gave me food. Your kindness is greater than the mountains and like the blessing that first brought me into life. Though my soul is by no means perfect, I long for some way by which to requite your favor, and so I have exercised my powers on your behalf. Your present journey is for the purpose of trying the official examination, so I shall tell you beforehand what the form is to be, and the subject. It is to be of character groups of fives, in couplets; the rhyme sound is 'pong,' and the subject 'Peaks and Spires of the Summer Clouds.' I have already composed one for you, which, if you care to use it, will undoubtedly win you the first place. It is this:

> The white sun rode high up in the heavens,
> And the floating clouds formed a lofty peak;
> The priest who saw them asked if there was a temple
> there,
> And the crane lamented the fact that no pines were
> visible;
> But the lightning from the cloud was the flashings of
> the woodsman's axe,
> And the muffled thunder was the bell calls of the
> holy temple.
> Will any say that the hills do not move?
> On the sunset breezes they sailed away.

After thus stating it, he bowed and took his departure.

The man, in wonder, awakened from his dream, came up to Seoul, and behold, the subject was as foretold by the spirit. He wrote what had been given him and became first in the honors of the occasion.

TEN THOUSAND DEVILS

A certain Prince Han of Chungcheong-do had a distant relative who was an uncouth countryman living in extreme poverty. This relative came to visit him from time to time. Han pitied his cold and hungry condition, gave him clothes to wear, and shared his food, urging him to stay and prolong his visit often into several months. He felt sorry for him but disliked his uncouthness and stupidity.

On one of these visits the poor relation suddenly announced his intention to return home, although the New Year's season was just at hand. Han urged him to remain, saying, "It would be better for you to be comfortably housed at my home, eating cake and soup and enjoying quiet sleep, rather than riding through wind and weather at this season of the year."

He said at first that he would have to go, until his host so insistently urged on him to stay that at last he yielded and gave consent. At New Year's Eve he remarked to Prince Han, "I am possessor of a peculiar kind of magic, by which I have under my control all manner of evil genii, and New Year's is the season at which I call them up, run over their names, and inspect them. If I did not do so I should lose control altogether, and there would follow no end of trouble among mortals. It is a matter of no small moment, and that is why I wished to go. Since, however, you have detained me, I shall have to call them up in your Excellency's house and look them over. I hope you will not object."

Han was greatly astonished and alarmed but gave his consent. The poor relation went on to say further, "This is an extremely important matter, and I would like to have for it your central guest hall."

Han consented to this also, so that night they washed the floors and scoured them clean. The relation also sat himself with all dignity facing the south, while Prince Han took up his station on the outside prepared to spy. Soon he saw a startling variety of demons crushing in at the door, horrible in appearance and awesome of manner. They lined up one after another, and still another, and another, till they filled the entire court, each bowing as he came before the master, who, at this point, drew out a book, opened it before him, and began calling off the names. Demon guards who stood by the threshold repeated the call and checked off the names just as they do in a government yamen. From the second watch it went on till the fifth of the morning. Han remarked, "It was indeed no lie when he told me 'ten thousand devils.'"

One latecomer arrived after the marking was over, and still another came climbing over the wall. The man ordered them to be arrested, and inquiry was made of them under the paddle. The late arrival said, "I really have had a hard time of it of late to live and so was obliged, in order to find anything, to inject smallpox into the home of a scholar who lives in Yeongnam. It is a long way off, and so I have arrived too late for the roll call, a serious fault indeed, I confess."

The one who climbed the wall said, "I, too, have known want and hunger and so had to insert a little typhus into the family of a gentleman who lives in Gyeonggi-do, but hearing that roll call was due, I came helter-skelter, fearing lest I should arrive too late, and so climbed the wall, which was indeed a sin."

The man then, in a loud voice, rated them soundly, saying, "These devils have disobeyed my orders, caused disease, and sinned grievously. Worse than everything, they have climbed the wall of a high official's house." He ordered a hundred blows to be given them with the paddle, the cangue to be put on, and to have them locked fast in prison. Then, calling the others to him, he said, "Do not spread disease! Do you understand?" Three times he ordered it and five times he repeated it. Then they were all dismissed. The crowd of devils lined off before him, taking their departure and crushing out through the gate with no end of noise and confusion. After a long time, they had all disappeared.

Prince Han, looking on during this time, saw the man now seated alone in the hall. It was quiet, and all had vanished. The cocks crowed and morning came. Han was astonished above measure and asked as to the law that governed such work as this. The poor relation said in reply, "When I was young I studied in a monastery in the mountains. In that monastery was an old priest who had a most peculiar countenance. A man feeble and ready to die, he seemed. All the priests made sport of him and treated him with contempt. I alone had pity on his age, and often gave him of my food and always treated him kindly. One evening, when the moon was bright, the old priest said to me, 'There is a cave behind this monastery from which a beautiful view may be had; will you not come with me and share it?'

"I went with him, and when we crossed the ridge of the hills into the stillness of the night he drew a book from his breast and gave it to me, saying, 'I, who am old and ready to die, have here a great secret, which I have long wished to pass on to someone worthy. I have traveled over the wide length of Korea and have never found the man till now I meet you, and my heart is satisfied, so please receive it.'

"I opened the book and found it a catalog list of devils, with magic writing interspersed, and an explanation of the laws that govern the spirit world. The old priest wrote out one magic recipe and, having set fire to it, countless devils at once assembled, at which I was greatly alarmed. He then sat with me and called over the names, one after the other, and said to the devils, 'I am an old man now, am going away, and so am about to put you under the care of this young man; obey him and all will be well.'

"I already had the book and so called them to me, read out the new orders, and dismissed them.

"The old priest and I returned to the temple and went to sleep. I awoke early next morning and went to call on him, but he was gone. Thus I came into possession of the magic art and have possessed it for a score of years and more. What the world knows nothing of I have thus made known to your Excellency."

Han was astonished beyond measure and asked, "May I not also come into possession of this wonderful gift?"

The man replied, "Your Excellency has great ability and can do wonderful things, but the possessor of this craft must be one poor and despised, and of no account. For you, a minister, it would never do."

The next day he left suddenly, and returned no more. Han sent a servant with a message to him. The servant, with great difficulty, at last found him alone among a thousand mountain peaks, living in a little straw hut no bigger than a cockle shell. No neighbors were there, nor any one beside. He called him, but he refused to come. He sent another messenger to invite him, but he had moved away and no trace of him was left.

THE HOME OF THE FAIRIES

In the days of King Injo (1623–1649) there was a student of Confucius who lived in Gapyeong. He was still a young man and unmarried. His education had not been extensive, for he had read only a little in the way of history and literature. For some reason or other he left his home and went into Gangwon-do. Traveling on horseback and with a servant, he reached a mountain, where he was overtaken by rain that wet him through. Mysteriously, from some unknown cause, his servant suddenly died, and the man, in fear and distress, drew the body to the side of the hill, where he left it and went on his way, weeping. When he had gone but a short distance, the horse he rode fell under him and died also.

Such was his plight: his servant dead, his horse dead, rain falling fast, and the road an unknown one. He did not know what to do or where to go, and reduced thus to walking, he broke down and cried. At this point there met him an old man with very wonderful eyes and hair as white as snow. He asked the young man why he wept, and the reply was that his servant was dead, his horse was dead, that it was raining, and that he did not know the way. The patriarch, on hearing this, took pity on him and, lifting his staff, pointed, saying, "There is a house yonder, just beyond those pines; follow that stream and it will bring you to where there are people."

The young man looked as directed, and a *li** or so beyond he saw a clump of trees. He bowed, thanked the stranger, and started on his way. When he had gone a few paces he looked back, but the friend had disappeared. Greatly wondering, he went on toward the place indicated, and as he drew near he saw a grove of pines, huge trees they were, a whole forest of them. Bamboos appeared, too, in countless numbers, with a wide stream of water flowing by. Underneath the water there seemed to be marble flooring, like a great pavement, white and pure. As he went along he saw that the water was all of an even depth, such as one could cross easily. A mile or

---

* A unit of distance. One *li* is approximately 0.393 km.

so farther on, he saw a beautifully decorated house. The pillars and entrance approaches were perfect in form. He continued his way, wet as he was, carrying his thorn staff, and entered the gate and sat down to rest. It was paved, too, with marble, and smooth as polished glass. There were no chinks or creases in it; all was of one perfect surface. In the room was a marble table, and on it a copy of the *Book of Changes*; there was also a brazier of jade just in front. Incense was burning in it, and the fragrance filled the room. Beside these, nothing else was visible. The rain had ceased and all was quiet and clear, with no wind or anything to disturb. The world of confusion seemed to have receded from him.

While he sat there, looking in astonishment, he suddenly heard the sound of footfalls from the rear of the building. Startled by it, he turned to see when an old man appeared. He looked as though he might equal the turtle or the crane in age and was very dignified. He wore a green dress and carried a jade staff of nine sections. The appearance of the old man was such as to stun any inhabitant of the earth. He recognized him as the master of the place, and so he went forward and made a low obeisance.

The old man received him kindly and said, "I am the master and have long waited for you." He took him by the hand and led him away. As they went along, the hills grew more and more enchanting, while the soft breezes and the light touched him with mystifying favor. Suddenly, as he looked, the man was gone, so he went on by himself and arrived soon at another palace built likewise of precious stones. It was a great hall, stretching on into the distance as far as the eye could see.

The young man had seen the Royal Palace frequently when in Seoul attending examinations, but compared with this, the Royal Palace was as a mud hut thatched with straw.

As he reached the gate, a man in ceremonial robes received him and led him in. He passed two or three pavilions and at last reached a special one and went up to the upper story. There, reclining at a table, he saw the ancient sage whom he had met before. Again he bowed.

This young man, brought up poorly in the country, was never accustomed to seeing or dealing with the great. In fear, he did not dare to lift his eyes. The ancient master, however, again welcomed him and asked him to be seated, saying, "This is not the dusty world that you are accustomed to but the abode of the genii. I knew you were coming and so was waiting to receive you." He turned and called, saying, "Bring something for the guest to eat."

In a little while a servant brought a richly laden table. It was such fare as was never seen on earth, and there was an abundance of it. The young man, hungry as he was, ate heartily of these strange viands. Then the dishes were carried away and the old man said, "I have a daughter who has arrived at a marriageable age, and I have been trying to find a son-in-law but as yet have not succeeded. Your coming accords with this need. Live here, then, and become my son-in-law." The young man, not knowing what to think, bowed and was silent. Then the host turned and gave an order, saying, "Call in the children."

Two boys about twelve or thirteen years of age came running in and sat down beside him. Their faces were so beautifully white they seemed like jewels. The master pointed to them and said to the guest, "These are my sons," and to the sons he said, "This young man is he whom I have chosen for my son-in-law; when should we have the wedding? Choose you a lucky day and let me know."

The two boys reckoned over the days on their fingers and then together said, "The day after tomorrow is a lucky day."

The old man, turning to the stranger, said, "That decides as to the wedding, and now you must wait in the guestchamber till the time arrives." He then gave a command to call so-and-so. In a little an official of the genii came forward, dressed in light and airy garments. His appearance and expression were very beautiful, a man, he seemed, of glad and happy mien.

The master said, "Show this young man the way to

his apartments and treat him well till the time of the wedding."

The official then led the way, and the young man bowed as he left the room. When he had passed outside the gate, a red sedan chair was in waiting for him. He was asked to mount. Eight bearers bore him smoothly along. A mile or so distant they reached another palace, equally wonderful, with no speck or flaw of any kind to mar its beauty. In graceful groves of flowers and trees he descended to enter his pavilion. Beautiful garments were taken from jeweled boxes, and a perfumed bath was given him and a change made. Thus he laid aside his weather-beaten clothes and donned the vestments of the genii. The official remained as company for him till the appointed time.

When that day arrived, other beautiful robes were brought, and again he bathed and changed. When he was dressed, he mounted the palanquin and rode to the palace of the master, twenty or more officials accompanying. On arrival, a guide directed them to the special Palace Beautiful. Here he saw preparations for the wedding, and here he made his bow. This finished, he moved as directed, further in. The tinkling sound of jade bells and the breath of sweet perfumes filled the air. Thus he made his entry into the inner quarters.

Many beautiful women were in waiting, all gorgeously appareled, like the women of the gods. Among these he imagined that he would meet the master's daughter. In a little, accompanied by a host of others, she came, shining in jewels and beautiful clothing so that she lit up the palace. He took his stand before her, though her face was hidden from him by a fan of pearls. When he saw her at last, so beautiful was she that his eyes were dazzled. The other women, compared with her, were as the magpie to the phoenix. So bewildered was he that he dared not look up. The friend accompanying assisted him to bow and to go through the necessary forms. The ceremony was much the same as that observed among men. When it was over the young man went back to his bridegroom's chamber. There, the embroidered curtains, the golden screens, the silken clothing, the jeweled floor, were such as no men of earth ever see.

On the second day his mother-in-law called him to her. Her age would be about thirty, and her face was like a freshly blown lotus flower. Here a great feast was spread, with many guests invited. The accompaniments thereof in the way of music were sweeter than mortals ever dreamed of. When the feast was over, the women caught up their skirts, and, lifting their sleeves, danced together and sang in sweet accord. The sound of their singing caused even the clouds to stop and listen. When the day was over and all had well dined, the feast broke up.

A young man, brought up in a country hut, had all of

a sudden met the chief of the genii and come to share in his glory and the accompaniments of his life. His mind was dazed and his thoughts overcame him. Doubts were mixed with fears. He knew not what to do.

A sharer in the joys of the fairies he had actually become, and a year or so passed in such delight as no words can ever describe.

One day his wife said to him, "Would you like to enter into the inner enclosure and see as the fairies see?"

He replied, "Gladly would I."

She then led him into a special park where there were lovely walks, surrounded by green hills. As they advanced there were charming views, with springs of water and sparkling cascades. The scene grew gradually more entrancing, with jeweled flowers and scintillating spray, lovely birds and animals disporting themselves. Once entering here, a man would never again think of earth as a place to return to.

After seeing this, he ascended the highest peak of all, which was like a tower of many stories. Before him lay a wide stretch of sea, with islands of the blessed standing out of the water and long stretches of pleasant land in view. His wife showed them all to him, pointing out this and that. They seemed filled with golden palaces and surrounded with a halo of light. They were peopled with happy souls, some riding on cranes, some on the phoenix, some on the unicorn; some were sitting on the clouds, some sailing by on the wind, some walking on the air, some gliding gently up the streams, some descending from above, some ascending, some moving west, some north, some gathering in groups. Flutes and harps sounded sweetly. So many and so startling were the things seen that he could never tell the tale of them. After the day had passed, they returned.

Thus was their joy unbroken, and when two years had gone by she bore him two sons.

Time moved on when one day, unexpectedly, as he was seated with his wife, he began to cry and tears soiled his face. She asked in amazement for the cause of it. "I was thinking," said he, "of how a plain countryman living in poverty had thus become the son-in-law of the king of the genii. But in my home is my poor old mother, whom I have not seen for these years; I would so like to see her that my tears flow."

The wife laughed, and said, "Would you really like to see her? Then go, but do not cry." She told her father that her husband would like to go and see his mother. The master called him and gave his permission. The son thought, of course, that he would call many servants and send him in state, but it was not so. His wife gave him one little bundle and that was all; so he said good-bye to his father-in-law, whose parting word was, "Go now and see your mother, and in a little I shall call for you again."

He sent with him one servant, and so he passed out

through the main gateway. There he saw a poor thin horse with a worn rag of a saddle on his back. He looked carefully and found that they were the dead horse and the dead servant, whom he had lost, restored to him. He gave a start and asked, "How did you come here?"

The servant answered, "I was coming with you on the road when someone caught me away and brought me here. I did not know the reason, but I have been here for a long time."

The man, in great fear, fastened on his bundle and started on his journey. The genie servant brought up the rear, but after a short distance the world of wonder had become transformed into the old weary world again. Here it was with its fogs, thorn, and precipice. He looked off toward the world of the genii, and it was but a dream. So overcome was he by his feelings that he broke down and cried.

The genie servant said to him when he saw him weeping, "You have been for several years in the abode of the immortals, but you have not yet attained thereto, for you have not yet forgotten the seven things of earth: anger, sorrow, fear, ambition, hate, and selfishness.* If you get rid of these, there will be no tears for you." On hearing this he stopped his crying, wiped his cheeks, and

* The original translation was also missing one of the seven.

asked pardon.

When he had gone a mile farther, he found himself on the main road. The servant said to him, "You know the way from this point on, so I shall go back," and thus at last the young man reached his home.

He found there an exorcising ceremony in progress. Shamans and spirit worshippers had been called and were saying their prayers. The family, seeing the young man come home thus, were all aghast. "It is his ghost," said they. However, they saw in a little that it was really he himself. The mother asked why he had not come home in all that time. She being a very violent woman in disposition, he did not dare to tell her the truth, so he made up something else. The day of his return was the anniversary of his supposed death, and so they had called the shamans for a prayer ceremony. Here he opened the bundle that his wife had given him and found four suits of clothes, one for each season.

About a year after his return home, the mother, seeing him alone, made application for the daughter of one of the village literati. The man, being timid by nature and afraid of offending his mother, did not dare to refuse and was therefore married, but there was no joy in it, and the two never looked at each other.

The young man had a friend whom he had known intimately from childhood. After his return, the friend came to see him frequently, and they used to spend the nights talking together. In their talks the friend inquired why in all these years he had never come home. The young man then told him what had befallen him in the land of the genii, and how he had been there and had been married. The friend looked at him in wonder, for he seemed just as he had remembered him except in the matter of clothing. This, he found on examination, was of very strange material, neither grass cloth, silk, nor cotton, but different from them all, and yet warm and comfortable. When spring came, the spring clothes sufficed, when summer came, those for summer, and for autumn and winter each special suit. They were never washed and yet never became soiled; they never wore out and always looked fresh and new. The friend was greatly astonished.

Some three years passed when one day there came once more a servant from the master of the genii, bringing his two sons. There were also letters that said, "Next year the place where you dwell will be destroyed and all the people will become 'fish and meat' for the enemy, therefore follow this messenger and come, all of you."

He told his friend of this and showed him his two sons. The friend, when he saw these children that looked like silk and jade, confessed the matter to the mother also. She, too, gladly agreed, and so they sold out, had a great feast for all the people of the town, and then bade farewell. This was the year 1635. They left and were never heard of again. The year following was the Manchu invasion, when the village where the young man had lived was all destroyed. To this day young and old in Gapyeong tell this story.

THE SNAKE'S REVENGE

There lived in ancient days an archer whose home was near the Water Gate of Seoul. He was a man of great strength and famous for his valor.

Water Gate has reference to a hole under the city wall by which the waters of the Grand Canal find their exit. In it are iron pickets to prevent people's entering or departing by that way.

On a certain afternoon when this military officer was taking a walk, a great snake was seen making its way by means of the Water Gate. The snake's head had already passed between the bars, but its body, being larger, could not get through, so there it was held fast. The soldier drew an arrow and, fitting it into the string, shot the snake in the head. Its head being fatally injured, the creature died. The archer then drew it out, pounded it into a pulp, and left it.

A little time later the man's wife conceived and bore a son. From the first the child was afraid of its father, and when it saw him it used to cry and seem greatly frightened. As it grew, it hated the sight of its father more and more. The man became suspicious of this, and so, instead of loving his son, he grew to dislike him.

On a certain day, when there were just the two of them in the room, the officer lay down to have a midday siesta, covering his face with his sleeve, but all the while keeping his eye on the boy to see what he would do. The child glared at his father and, thinking him asleep, got a knife and made a thrust at him. The man jumped, grabbed the knife, and then with a club gave the boy a blow that left him dead on the spot. He pounded him into a pulp, left him, and went away. The mother, however, in tears, covered the little form with a quilt and prepared for its burial. In a little the quilt began to move, and she, in alarm, raised it to see what had happened, when lo! beneath it the child was gone and there lay coiled a huge snake instead. The mother jumped back in fear, left the room, and did not again enter.

When evening came, the husband returned and heard the dreadful story from his wife. He went in and looked, and saw it had metamorphosed into a huge snake. On the head of it was the scar of the arrow that he had shot. He said to the snake, "You and I were originally not enemies, I therefore did wrong in shooting you as I did, but your intention to take revenge through becoming my son was a horrible deed. Such a thing as this is proof that my suspicions of you were right and just. You became my son in order to kill me, your father; why, therefore, should I not in my turn kill you? If you attempt it again, it will certainly end in my taking your life. You have already had your revenge, and have once more transmigrated into your original shape; let us drop the past and be friends from now on. What do you say?"

He repeated this over and urged his proposals, while the snake, with bowed head, seemed to listen intently. He then opened the door and said, "Now you may go as you please." The snake then departed, making straight for the Water Gate, and passed out between the bars. It did not again appear.

THE BRAVE MAGISTRATE

In olden times in one of the counties of North Hamgyeong-do there was an evil-smelling goblin that caused great destruction to life. Successive magistrates appeared, but in ten days or so after arrival, in each case they died in great agony, so that no man wished to have the billet or anything to do with the place. A hundred or more were asked to take the post, but they all refused. At last, one brave soldier, who was without any influence socially or politically, accepted. He was a courageous man, strong and fearless. He thought, "Even though there is a devil there, all men will not die, surely. I shall make a trial of him." So he said his farewell and entered on his office. He found himself alone in the yamen, as all others had taken flight. He constantly carried a long knife at his belt and went thus armed, for he noticed from the first day a fishy, stinking odor that grew gradually more and more marked.

After five or six days he took note, too, that what looked like a mist would frequently make its entry by the outer gate, and from this mist came this stinking smell. Daily it grew more and more annoying, so that he could not stand it longer. In ten days or so, when the time arrived for him to die, the yamen-runners and servants, who had returned, again ran away. The magistrate kept a jar of whisky by his side, from which he drank frequently to fortify his soul. On this day he grew very drunk, and thus waited. At last he saw something coming through the main gateway that seemed wrapped in fog, three or four embraces in waist size and fifteen feet or so high. There was no head to it, nor were body or arms visible. Only on the top were two dreadful eyes rolling wildly. The magistrate jumped up at once, rushed toward it, gave a great shout, and struck it with his sword. When he gave it the blow, there was the sound of thunder, and the whole thing dissipated. Also, the foul smell that accompanied it disappeared at once.

The magistrate then, in a fit of intoxication, fell prone. The retainers, all thinking him dead, gathered in the courtyard to prepare for his burial. They saw him fallen to the earth, but they remarked that the bodies of others who had died from this evil had all been left on the veranda, but his was in the lower court. They raised him up in order to prepare him for burial when, suddenly, he came to life, looked at them in anger, and asked what they meant. Fear and amazement possessed them. From that time on there was no more smell.

THE KING OF HELL

In Yeonan County, Hwanghae-do, there was a certain literary graduate whose name I have forgotten. He fell ill one day and remained in his room, leaning helplessly against his armrest. Suddenly, several spirit soldiers appeared to him, saying, "The Governor of the lower hell has ordered your arrest," so they bound him with a chain about his neck and led him away. They journeyed for many hundreds of miles and at last reached a place that had a very high wall. The spirits then took him within the walls, and they went on for a long distance.

There was within this enclosure a great structure whose height reached to heaven. They arrived at the gate, and the spirits who had him in hand led him in, and when they entered the inner courtyard, they laid him down on his face.

Glancing up, he saw what looked like a king seated on a throne; grouped about him on each side were attendant officers. There were also scores of secretaries and soldiers going and coming on pressing errands. The King's appearance was most terrible, and his commands such as to fill one with awe. The graduate felt the perspiration break out on his back, and he dared not look up. In a little, a secretary came forward and stood in front of the raised dais to transmit commands from the King, who had asked, "Where do you come from? What is your name? How old are you? What do you do for a living? Tell me the truth now, and no dissembling."

The scholar, frightened to death, replied, "My clan name is so-and-so, and my given name is so and-so. I am so old, and I have lived for several generations at Yeonan, Hwanghae-do. I am stupid and ill-equipped by nature so have not done anything special. I have heard all my life that if you say your beads with love and pity in your heart, you will escape hell, and so have given my time to calling on the Buddha and dispensing alms."

The secretary, hearing this, went at once and reported it to the King. After some time he came back with a message, saying, "Come up closer to the steps, for you are not the person intended. It happens that you bear the same name and you have thus been wrongly arrested. You may go now."

The scholar joined his hands and made a deep bow. Again the secretary transmitted a message from the King, saying, "My house, when on earth, was in such a place in such and such a ward of Seoul. When you go back I want to send a message by you. My coming here is long, and the outer coat I wear is worn to shreds. Ask my people to send me a new outercoat. If you do so, I shall be greatly obliged, so see that you do not forget."

The scholar said, "Your Majesty's message given me thus direct I shall pass on without fail, but the ways of the two worlds, the dark world and the light, are so different that when I give the message the hearers will say I am talking nonsense. True, I'll give it just as you have commanded, but what about it if they refuse to listen? I ought to have some evidence as proof to help me out."

The King made answer, "Your words are true, very true. This will help you: When I was on earth," said he, "one of my head buttons that I wore had a broken edge, and I hid it in the third volume of the *Book of History*. I alone know of it, no one else in the world. If you give this as a proof, they will listen."

The scholar replied, "That will be satisfactory, but again, how shall I do in case they make the new coat?"

The reply was, "Prepare a sacrifice, offer the coat by fire, and it will reach me."

He then bade good-bye, and the King sent with him two soldier guards. He asked the soldiers, as they came out, who the one seated on the throne was. "He is the King of Hades," said they. "His surname is Pak and his given name is U."

They arrived at the bank of a river, and the two soldiers pushed him into the water. He awoke with a start and found that he had been dead for three days.

When he recovered from his sickness, he came up to Seoul, searched out the house indicated, and made careful inquiry as to the name, finding that it was no other than Pak U. Pak U had two sons, who at that time had graduated and were holding office. The graduate wanted to see the sons of this King of Hades, but the gatekeeper would not let him in. Therefore he stood before the red gate waiting helplessly till the sun went down. Then came out from the inner quarters of the house an old servant, to whom he earnestly made petition that he might see the master. On being thus requested, the servant returned and reported it to the master, who, a little later, ordered him in. On entering, he saw two gentlemen who seemed to be chiefs. They had him sit down and then questioned him as to who he was and what he had to say.

He replied, "I am a student living in Yeonan County, Hwanghae-do. On such and such a day I died and went into the other world, where your honorable father gave me such and such a commission."

The two listened for a little and then, without waiting

to hear all that he had to say, grew very angry and began to scold him, saying, "How dare such a scarecrow as you come into our house and say such things as these? This is stuff and nonsense that you talk. Pitch him out," they shouted to the servants.

He, however, called back saying, "I have a proof; listen. If it fails, why then, pitch me out."

One of the two said, "What possible proof can you have?" Then the scholar told, with great exactness and care, the story of the head button.

The two, in astonishment over this, had the book taken down and examined, and sure enough in Vol. III of the *Book of History* was the button referred to. Not a single particular had failed. It proved to be a button that they had missed after the death of their father, and that they had searched for in vain.

Accepting the message now as true, they all entered upon a period of mourning. The women of the family also called in the scholar and asked him specially of what he had seen. So they made the outercoat, chose a day, and offered it by fire before the ancestral altar. Three days after the sacrifice the scholar dreamed, and the family of Pak dreamed too, that the King of Hades had come and given to each one of them his thanks for the coat. They long kept the scholar at their home, treating him with great respect, and became his firm friends for ever after.

Hong's Experiences
in Hades

Hong Nae-Beom was a military graduate who was born in the year 1561 and lived in the city of Pyongyang. He passed his examination in the year 1603, and in the year 1637 attained to the Third Degree. He was 82 in the year 1643, and his son Seon memorialized the King asking that his father be given rank appropriate to his age. At that time a certain Han Hyeong-gil was chief of the Royal Secretaries, and he refused to pass on the request to his Majesty. But in the year 1644, when the Crown Prince was returning from his exile in China, he came by way of Pyongyang. Seon took advantage of this to present the same request to the Crown Prince. His Highness received it and had it brought to the notice of the King. In consequence, Hong received the rank of Second Degree.

On receiving it he said, "This year I shall die," and a little later he died.

In the year 1594, Hong fell ill of typhus fever, and after ten days of suffering, died. They prepared his body for burial and placed it in a coffin. Then the friends and relatives left, and his wife remained alone in charge. All of a sudden the body turned itself and fell to the ground with a thud. The woman, frightened, fainted away, and the other members of the family came rushing to her help. From this time on, the body resumed its functions, and Hong lived.

Said he, "In my dream I went to a certain region, a place of great fear where many persons were standing around, as well as awful ogres, some of them wearing bulls' heads and some with faces of wild beasts. They crowded about and jumped and pounced toward me in all directions. A scribe robed in black sat on a platform and addressed me, saying, 'There are three religions on earth: Confucianism, Buddhism, and Taoism. According to Buddhism, you know that heaven and hell are places that decide between man's good and evil deeds. You have ever been a blasphemer of the Buddha and a denier of a future life, acting always as though you knew everything, blustering and storming. You are now to be sent to hell, and ten thousand kalpas will not see you out of it.'

"Then, two or three constables carrying spears came and took me off. I screamed, 'You are wrong, I am innocently condemned.' Just at that moment, a certain Buddha, with a face of shining gold, came smiling toward me and said, 'There is truly a mistake somewhere; this man must attain to the age of eighty-three and become an officer of the Second Degree ere he dies.' Then, addressing me, he asked, 'How is it that you have come here? The order was that a certain Hong of Jeonju be arrested and brought, not you; but now that you have come, look about the place before you go and tell the world afterwards of what you have seen.'

"The guards, on hearing this, took me in hand and brought me first to a prison house, where a sign was posted up marked, 'Stirrers Up of Strife.' I saw in this prison a great brazier-shaped pit, built of stones and filled with fire. Flames arose and forked tongues. The stirrers up of strife were taken and made to sit close before it. I then saw one infernal guard take a long rod of iron, heat it red-hot, and put out the eyes of the guilty ones. I saw also that the offenders were hung up like dried fish. The guides who accompanied me, said, 'While these were on earth, they did not love their brethren, but looked at others as enemies. They scoffed at the laws of God and sought only selfish gain, so they are punished.'

"The next hell was marked, 'Liars.' In that hell I saw an iron pillar of several yards in height, and great stones were placed before it. The offenders were called up and made to kneel before the pillar.

"Then I saw an executioner take a knife and drive a hole through the tongues of the offenders, pass an iron chain through each, and hang them to the pillar so that they dangled by their tongues several feet from the ground. A stone was then taken and tied to each culprit's feet. The stones thus bearing down, and the chains being fast to the pillar, their tongues were pulled out a foot or more, and their eyes rolled in their sockets. Their agonies were appalling. The guides again said, 'These offenders, when on earth, used their tongues skillfully to tell lies and separate friend from friend, and so they are punished.'

"The next hell had inscribed on it, 'Deceivers.' I saw in it many scores of people. There were ogres that cut the flesh from their bodies and fed it to starving demons. These ate and ate, and the flesh was cut and cut till only the bones remained. When the winds of hell blew, flesh returned to them; then, metal snakes and copper dogs crowded in to bite them and suck their blood. Their screams of pain made the earth tremble. The guides said to me, 'When these offenders were on earth, they held high office, and while they pretended to be true and good they received bribes in secret and were doers of all evil. As Ministers of State, they ate the fat of the land and sucked the blood of the people, and yet advertised themselves as benefactors and were highly applauded. While in reality they lived as thieves, they pretended to be holy, as Confucius and Mencius are holy. They were deceivers of the world, and robbers, and so are punished thus.'

"The guides then said, 'It is not necessary that you see all the hells.' They said to one another, 'Let's take him yonder and show him.' So they went some distance to the southeast. There was a great house with a sign painted thus, 'The Home of the Blessed.' As I looked, there were beautiful halos encircling it, and clouds of glory. There were hundreds of monks in cassock and surplice. Some carried fresh-blown lotus flowers; some were seated like the Buddha; some were reading prayers.

"The guides said, 'These, when on earth, kept the faith, and with undivided hearts served the Buddha, and so have escaped the Eight Sorrows and the Ten Punishments,* and are now in the home of the happy, which is called heaven.' When we had seen all these things we returned.

"The golden-faced Buddha said to me, 'Not many on earth believe in the Buddha, and few know of heaven and hell. What do you think of it?'

"I bowed low and thanked him.

---

* Of the various trials and tribulations that people face during their lives in the Buddhist tradition, these are the ones that people must free themselves of.

"Then the black-coated scribe said, 'I am sending this man away; see him safely off.' The spirit soldiers took me with them, and while on the way I awakened with a start and found that I had been dead for four days."

Hong's mind was filled with pride on this account, and he frequently boasted of it. His age and Second Degree of rank came about just as the Buddha had predicted.

His experience, alas, was used as a means to deceive people, for the Superior Man does not talk of these strange and wonderful things.

Yi Tan, a Chinaman of the Song Kingdom, used to say, "If there is no heaven, there is no heaven, but if there is one, the Superior Man alone can attain to it. If there is no hell, there is no hell, but if there is one the bad man must inherit it."

If we examine Hong's story, while it looks like a yarn to deceive the world, it really is a story to arouse one to right action. I, Im Bang, have recorded it like Tuizhi,* saying, "Don't find fault with the story, but learn its lesson."

---

* The pen name of Han Yu, a Chinese writer and Neo-Confucian scholar during the Tang Dynasty.

TA-HONG

Minister Sim Hui-su was, when young, handsome as polished marble and white as the snow, rarely and beautifully formed. When eight years of age, he was already an adept at Chinese characters and a wonder in the eyes of his people. The boy's nickname was Sindong (the godlike one). After the passing of his first examination, he advanced step by step till at last he became First Minister of the land. When old, he was honored as the most renowned of all ministers. At seventy he still held office, and one day, when occupied with the affairs of State, he suddenly said to those about him, "Today is my last on earth, and my farewell wishes to you all are that you may prosper and do bravely and well."

His associates replied in wonder, "Your Excellency is still strong and hearty, and able for many years of work; why do you speak so?"

Sim laughingly made answer, "Our span of life is fixed. Why should I not know? We cannot pass the predestined limit. Please feel no regret. Use all your efforts to serve His Majesty the King and make grateful acknowledgment of his many favors."

Thus he exhorted them and took his departure. Everyone wondered over this strange announcement. From that day on he returned no more, it being said that he was ailing.

There was at that time attached to the War Office a young secretary directly under Sim. Hearing that his master was ill, the young man went to pay his respects and to make inquiry. Sim called him into his private room, where all was quiet. Said he, "I am about to die, and this is a long farewell, so take good care of yourself and do your part honorably."

The young man looked, and in Sim's eyes were tears. He said, "Your Excellency is still vigorous, and even though you are slightly ailing, there is surely no cause for anxiety. I am at a loss to understand your tears and what you mean by saying that you are about to die. I would like to ask the reason."

Sim smiled and said, "I have never told any person, but since you ask and there is no longer cause for concealment, I shall tell you the whole story. When I was young, certain things happened in my life that may make you smile.

"At about sixteen years of age I was said to be a handsome boy and fair to see. Once in Seoul, when a banquet was in progress and many dancing girls and other representatives of good cheer were called, I went too, with a half-dozen comrades, to see. There was among the dancing girls a young woman whose face was very beautiful. She was not like an earthly person, but like some angelic being. Inquiring as to her name, some of those seated near said it was Ta-hong (Flower Bud).

"When all was over and the guests had separated, I went home, but I thought of Ta-hong's pretty face and recalled her repeatedly, over and over; seemingly, I could not forget her. Ten days or so later, I was returning from my teacher's house along the main street, carrying my books under my arm, when I suddenly met a pretty girl, who was beautifully dressed and riding a handsome horse. She alighted just in front of me and, to my surprise, taking my hand, said, 'Are you not Sim Hui-su?'

"In my astonishment, I looked at her and saw that it was Ta-hong. I said, 'Yes, but how do you know me?' I was not married then, nor had I my hair done up, and as there were many people in the street looking on, I was very much ashamed. Flower Bud, with a look of gladness in her face, said to her pony-boy, 'I have something to see to just now; you return and say to the master that I shall be present at the banquet tomorrow.' Then we went aside into a neighboring house and sat down. She said, 'Did you not on such and such a day go to such and such a Minister's house and look on at the gathering?' I answered, 'Yes, I did.' 'I saw you,' said she, 'and to me your face was like a god's. I asked those present who you were, and they said your family name was Sim and your given name Hui-su, and that your character and gifts were very superior. From that day on I longed to meet you, but as there was no possibility of this I could only think of you. Our meeting thus is surely of God's appointment.'

"I replied laughingly, 'I, too, felt just the same towards you.'

"Then Ta-hong said, 'We cannot meet here; let's go to my aunt's home in the next ward, where it's quiet, and talk there.' We went to the aunt's home. It was neat and clean and somewhat isolated, and apparently the aunt loved Flower Bud with all the devotion of a mother. From that day forth we plighted our troth together. Flower Bud had never had a lover; I was her first and only choice. She said, however, 'This plan of ours cannot be consummated today; let us separate for the present and make plans for our union in the future.' I asked her how we could do so, and she replied, 'I have sworn my soul to you, and it is decided forever, but you have your parents to think of, and you have not yet had a wife chosen, so there will be no chance of their advising you to have a second wife as my social standing would require for me. As I reflect upon your ability and chances for promotion, I see you already a Minister of State. Let us separate just now, and I'll keep myself for you till the time when you win the first place at the examination and have your three days of public rejoicing. Then we'll meet once more. Let us make a compact never to be broken. So then, until you have won your honors, do not think of me, please. Do not be anxious, either, lest I should be taken from you, for I have a plan by which to hide myself away in safety. Know that on the day you win your honors we shall meet again.'

"On this we clasped hands and spoke our farewells as though we parted easily. Where she was going I did not ask, but simply came home with a distressed and burdened heart, feeling that I had lost everything. On my return I found that my parents, who had missed me, were in a terrible state of consternation, but so delighted were they at my safe return that they scarcely asked where I had been. I did not tell them either, but gave another excuse.

"At first I could not desist from thoughts of Ta-hong. After a long time only was I able to regain my composure. From that time forth I went at my lessons with all my might. Day and night I pegged away, not for the sake of the examination, but for the sake of once more meeting her.

"In two years or so my parents appointed my marriage. I did not dare to refuse and had to accept, but had no heart in it, and no joy in their choice.

"My gift for study was very marked, and by diligence I grew to be superior to all my competitors. It was five years after my farewell to Ta-hong that I won my honors. I was still but a youngster, and all the world rejoiced in my success. But my joy was in the secret understanding that the time had come for me to meet Ta-hong. On the first day of my graduation honors I expected to meet her, but did not. The second day passed, but I saw nothing of her, and the third day was passing and no word had reached me. My heart was so disturbed that I found not the slightest joy in the honors of the occasion. Evening was falling when my father said to me, 'I have a friend of my younger days, who now lives in Changui-dong, and you must go and call on him this evening before the three days are over,' and so, there being no help for it, I went to pay my call. As I was returning, the sun had gone down and it was dark, and just as I was passing a high gateway, I heard the *sillae* (a shrill whistle by which graduates command the presence of a new graduate to haze or honor, as they please) call. It was the home of an old Minister, a man whom I did not know, but he being a high noble there was nothing for me to do but dismount and enter. Here I found the master himself, an old gentleman, who put me through my humble exercises and then ordered me gently to come up and sit beside him. He talked to me very kindly and entertained me with all sorts of refreshments. Then he lifted his glass and inquired, 'Would you like to meet a very beautiful person?' I did not know what he meant and so asked, 'What beautiful person?' The old man said, 'The most beautiful in the world to you. She has long been a member of my household.' Then he ordered a servant to call her. When she came, it was my lost Ta-hong. I was startled, delighted, surprised, and almost speechless. 'How do you come here?' I gasped.

"She laughed and said, 'Is this not within the three days of your public celebration and according to the agreement by which we parted?'

"The old man said, 'She is a wonderful woman. Her thoughts are high and noble, and her history is quite unique. I will tell it to you. I am an old man of eighty, and my wife and I have had no children, but on a certain day this young girl came to us saying, "May I have the place of slave with you, to wait on you and do your bidding?"

"'In surprise I asked the reason for this strange request, and she said, "I am not running away from any master, so do not mistrust me."

"'Still, I did not wish to take her in and told her so, but she begged so persuasively that I yielded and let her stay, appointed her work to do, and watched her behavior. She became a slave of her own accord, and simply lived to please us: preparing our meals during the day and caring for our rooms for the night, responding to calls, ever ready to do our bidding, and faithful beyond compare. We feeble old folks, often ill, found her a source of comfort and cheer unheard of, making life perfect peace and joy. Her needle, too, was exceedingly skillful, and according to the seasons she prepared all that we needed. Naturally, we loved and pitied her more than I can say. My wife thought more of her than any mother did of a daughter. During the day she was always at hand, and at night she slept by her side. At one time I asked her quietly concerning her past history. She said she was originally the child of a freeman but that her parents had died when she was very young, and, having no place to go to, an old woman of the village had taken her in and brought her up. "Being so young," said she, "I was safe from harm. At last I met a young master with whom I plighted a hundred years of troth, a beautiful boy; none was ever like him. I determined to meet him again, but only after he had won his honors in the arena. If I had remained at the home of the old mother, I could not have kept myself safe and preserved my honor; I would have been helpless. So I came here for safety and to serve you. It is a plan by which to hide myself for a year or so, and then when he wins I shall ask your leave to go."

"'I then asked who the person was with whom she had made this contract, and she told me your name. I am so old that I no longer think of taking wives and concubines, but she called herself my concubine so as to be safe, and thus the years have passed. We watched the examination reports, but till this time your name was absent. Through it all she expressed not a single word of anxiety, but kept up heart saying that before long your name would appear. So confident was she that not a shadow of disappointment was in her face. This time on looking over the list, I found your name and told her. She heard it without any special manifestation of joy, saying she knew it would come. She also said, "When we parted I promised to meet him before the three days of public celebration were over, and now I must make good my promise." So she climbed to the upper pavilion to watch the public way. But this ward being somewhat remote, she did not see you going by on the first day, nor on the second. This morning she went again, saying, "He will surely pass today," and so it came about. She said, "He is coming; call him in."

"'I am an old man, and I have read much history and heard of many famous women. There are many examples of devotion that move the heart, but I never saw so faithful a life or one so devoted to another. God, taking note of this, has brought all her purposes to pass. And now, not to let this moment of joy go by, you must stay with me tonight.'

"When I met Ta-hong I was most happy, especially as I heard of her years of faithfulness. As to the invitation, I declined it, saying I could not think, even though we had so agreed, of taking away one who waited in attendance upon His Excellency. But the old man laughed, saying, 'She is not mine. I simply let her be called my concubine in name lest my nephews or some younger members of the clan should steal her away. She is first of all a faithful woman. I have not known her like before.'

"The old man then had the horse sent back and the servants, also a letter to my parents saying that I would stay the night. He ordered the servants to prepare a room, put in beautiful screens and embroidered matting, hang up lights, and decorate as for a bridegroom. Thus he celebrated our meeting.

"Next morning I bade good-bye, and I went and told my parents all about my meeting with Ta-hong and what had happened. They gave consent that I should have her, and she was brought and made a member of our family, really my only wife.

"Her life and behavior being beyond that of the ordinary, in serving those above her and in helping those below, she fulfilled all the requirements of the ancient code. Her work, too, was faithfully done, and her gifts in the way of music and chess* were most exceptional. I loved her as I never can tell.

"A little later I went as magistrate to Geumsan County in Jeolla-do and Ta-hong went with me. We were there for two years. She declined our too frequent happy times together, saying that it interfered with efficiency and duty. One day, all unexpectedly, she came to me and requested that we should have a little quiet time, with no others present, as she had something special to tell me. I asked her what it was, and she said to me, 'I am going to die, for my span of life is finished; so let us be glad once more and forget all the sorrows of the world.' I wondered when I heard this. I could not think it true and asked her how she could tell beforehand that she was going to die. She said, 'I know, there is no mistake about it.'

"In four or five days she fell ill, but not seriously, and yet a day or two later she died. She said to me when dying, 'Our life is ordered, God decides it all. While I lived I gave myself to you, and you most kindly responded in return. I have no regrets. As I die, I ask only that my body be buried where it may rest by the side of my master when he passes away, so that when we meet in the regions beyond I shall be with you once

---

* I.e., *janggi*, a Korean game similar to chess.

again.' When she had so said, she died.

"Her face was beautiful, not like the face of the dead, but like the face of the living. I was plunged into deepest grief and prepared her body with my own hands for burial. Our custom is that when a second wife dies, she is not buried with the family, but I made some excuse and had her interred in our family site in the county of Goyang. I did so to carry out her wishes. When I came as far as Geumgang River on my sad journey, I wrote a verse:

> O beautiful Bud, of the beautiful Flower,
> We bear thy form on the willow bier;
> Whither has gone thy sweet perfumed soul?
> The rains fall on us to tell us of thy tears and of thy
>   faithful way.

"I wrote this as a love tribute to my faithful Ta-hong. After her death, whenever anything serious was to happen in my home, she always came to tell me beforehand, and never was there a mistake in her announcements. For several years it has continued thus, till a few days ago she appeared in a dream saying, 'Master, the time of your departure has come, and we are to meet again. I am now making ready for your glad reception.'

"For this reason I have bidden all my associates

farewell. Last night she came once more and said to me, 'Tomorrow is your day.' We wept together in the dream as we met and talked. In the morning, when I awoke, marks of tears were still upon my cheeks. This is not because I fear to die, but because I have seen my Ta-hong. Now that you have asked me, I have told you all. Tell it to no one."

So Sim died, as was foretold, on the day following. Strange, indeed!

Credits

Publisher	Kim Hyung-geun
Editor	Kim Eugene
Copy Editor	Daisy Larios
Designer	Min So-young